Pride
&
Promiscuity

Good morning, Miss Bennet.

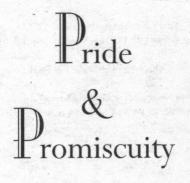

Pride & Promiscuity

The Lost Sex Scenes of Jane Austen

ARIELLE ECKSTUT

CANONGATE

*To David — my husband, my soul mate,
my true love*

First published in the UK in 2003 by
Canongate Books Ltd, 14 High Street, Edinburgh EH1 1TE

This edition published in 2004

First published in the United States of America by
Fireside, an imprint of Simon & Schuster, Inc.

1

British Library Cataloguing-in-Publication Data
A catalogue record for this book is available from the British
Library

ISBN 1 84195 582 5

Illustrated by Chris Brown

Typeset in Lapidary 333 BT by Elina D. Nudelman
Printed and bound by Clays Ltd, St Ives plc

www.canongate.net

Contents

CONTENTS

Preface

While suspended in amniotic fluid, I came to hear a familiar voice—that of a long-forgotten British stage actress reading the unabridged version of Emma on cassette tape. The story goes that when I was born, I had become so accustomed to and was so soothed by this recording that my parents used it as a pacifier whenever I became upset.

At the age of three, I began requesting which books I wanted read to me at bedtime. My three favorites were: *Ant & Bee*, *When We Were Very Young* and, of course, *Emma*. At five, I founded the Jane Austen Junior Appreciation League. And at ten, I organized dramatic readings of the entire Austen oeuvre, often performing all the characters myself.

My obsession with Austen continued through my school years and into college, where I majored in something called Fundamentals: Issues and Texts. It required me to choose a grand question which I was to support with six "great books" over four years of study. The six works were obvious: *Pride & Prejudice*, *Sense & Sensibility*, *Northanger Abbey*, *Emma*, *Mansfield Park*, and *Persuasion*.

Unfortunately, the graduate schools I applied to found my focus to be "too narrow" and I was denied admission to all 26 institutions to which I applied. Fortunately, my Uncle Elbert – a wealthy man with no immediate heirs and a singular love for Austen--encouraged me with kind words and a healthy stipend to pursue my scholarship on my own. I spent my days amassing a personal collection of authentic Austenian costumes (I am now the proud owner of the largest collection in Northern California). I spent my nights writing over 150 critical essays and articles on the great authoress (though none, as of yet, have been published).

When Uncle Elbert died, his books revealed that he was massively in debt and that he had quintuple-mortgaged his house. The news broke my heart and catapulted me into the job market, finding work as a literary agent and representing "books" whose mediocrity would have sent Jane to an even earlier death. I dearly missed my days spent with Austen's work and was delighted therefore to accept an invitation from an English friend to visit Herefordshire. Once again, I'd be able to sit and read all of Austen's novels uninterrupted.

The family had let for the week Shelwyck Court, a grand manor built over a period of five hundred years. Remarkably, a log had been kept that listed every visitor to the estate. The first evening was spent searching for famous guests. Eventually unfulfilled by the hunt, each of us picked a spot in the grand room upstairs, opened our books, and settled into a quiet evening by the fire. Until, that is, the host decided to open a window to rid the room of a smoky odor emanating from an imperfect flue. Despite a tremendous amount of effort, he was unable to push out the lead pane. I suggested trying another, but our host was determined. He made a point of saying he didn't care if it hadn't been opened in 186 years—he was going to fix the bloody thing. After much ado, the window finally cracked, followed by a crash. We hunted for the cause, but found nothing. Thus, we returned to our reading until, one by one, we retired for the night.

The following morning my host sent me to the garden to cut herbs for omelets. I was untangling my cuttings when I spied an antique wooden box. It lay beneath the aforementioned window, which had a small hole in the stone right below its sill. I suspected that all the maneuvering must have unsettled the box and sent it falling. Why such a thing was hidden in such a hole, I knew not, but my curiosity was positively piqued. The fall had unlatched the lock of the box to the point where all it needed was a quick, deft pull to unlatch it completely. Inside were pages covered with the exacting and graceful penmanship of a distinctly nineteenth-century hand. I took a number of papers and leaned up against Shelwyck Court's grand foundation and began to read.

What drama unfolded in my mind as truth overcame doubt cannot be expressed.

Suffice it to say that my life will be forever

divided in two: the moment prior to the realization that I had made one of the greatest literary discoveries of our time and the moment after I realized that kismet had showered its magic dust upon me. Through all my years of Austen obsession, I had never imagined *this*. Yes, I had had many fantastical scenarios swim through my head: finding the final scene of one of Jane's unfinished works; discovering unknown letters that gave a keener picture of her quiet domestic life; unearthing an early draft of *Emma* where Mr. Knightley dies an early death only to leave Emma distraught and single. But even these were silver to my pot of gold, baronets to my duke, Wickhams to my Darcy. Rather, I had in my hands the most scandalous, most outrageous writing, of which not one person could ever have guessed existed. The box contained Jane Austen's lost sex scenes. *Sex Scenes*. Along with letters to her editor and sister arguing and anguishing over the extensive cuts she was asked to make in order for her work to be acceptable and decent to her publisher.

While I had no advanced degree to prove

my instincts were correct, no published work to back my claim, I did have this: insight culled from dozens of readings of all of Austen's work, a thorough understanding of her voice in letters from reading each surviving epistle *ad infinitum*, and, lastly, the uniquely American naïveté to believe that the world was mine to discover.

Then came the clincher. On carefully re-examining Shelwyck Court's log during and just after the period of Jane's life, I saw that a Miss Cassie Austin had visited in May of 1818, near-ly one year after Jane's death. Just then a breeze blew the dot off the top of the "i" in Austin and I knew it could only be Jane's beloved sister, Cassandra. She must have come to this remote spot in order to deposit these remarkable pages to fate and time. That she wished them to be discovered, I can be quite sure, otherwise they would have been set to flames from the first. That she or, more importantly, that Jane Austen herself would wish them to be published, I do know: as stated clearly in the letters contained herein, Jane saw no shame in what she wrote and fully intended *all* her words to be read by the greatest number of people for all posterity.

Clearly, before I went public, I needed to have the imprimatur of a renowned Austen scholar in order to prove my instincts correct. Hence I approached Dr. Elfrida Drummond, the most conservative of all modern Austen scholars. I knew if I could obtain Dr. Drummond's stamp of authenticity, I was home free. Now it is my honor to present these scenes and letters together in one volume.

Arielle Eckstut
May 2003
San Rafael, CA

Introduction

In the autumn of 1999 I received a letter informing me of an important "discovery" concerning Jane Austen.

It was from an American, Arielle Eckstut, living in California and apparently eking out a living as some sort of lower-echelon literary hanger-on – agent and/or freelance writers. You can imagine the type, and will no doubt be unsurprised to learn that she was also a raging Anglophile, of the *Masterpiece Theatre*–watching, Typhoo-drinking sort.

Over the course of two decades as an Austen scholar, I have grown, if not exactly inured, at least somewhat familiar with these sorts of breathless announcements from total strangers. The people who made them were usually non-professional, and sometimes rather deranged, Austen fanatics who after spending years rereading *Pride and Prejudice* (or, more likely, watching the BBC miniseries version) had decided the novel was, in fact, a disguised allegory of the Life of Christ, or that Jane Austen was actually a homosexual man writing under a pseudonym, or some other such outré interpretation. In writing to me, a recognized Austen expert of some professional standing, they no doubt expected a scholarly, swift, and grateful confirmation of their insane ravings.

Without exception, I disappointed them. Quite apart from my simple disdain for groupies and crackpots, I am by temperament reluctant to credit "sensational" claims even by recognized academic scholars. My work for the last three decades has focused on Jane Austen's rhetorical strategies, chiefly her use of punctuation,[1] and I have little time for the sex/race/gender obsessions of the modern literature profession.

However, for reasons that are still not entirely clear even to me, I was intrigued by the American's note. After a number of messages back and forth, and against my better judgment, I arranged to have the manuscripts sent to me for analysis.

1.See, for example, E. Drummond, *Pride in Punctuation: Dashes, Semicolons, and Inverted Commas: Austenian Punctuation Conventions and Their Meaning* (Oxford: Oxford University Press, 1966).

I will not bore you here with a description of the months of difficult work that followed—the in-depth textual examination; analyses of the paper and ink used in the manuscripts; careful studies of the handwriting, dates, and other evidence that could be brought to bear on the subject.[2] I approached it all with the utmost skepticism. Quite apart from the healthy scholarly detachment appropriate to such an inquiry, I personally admit to wanting *not* to believe the manuscripts were genuine. If they were real, it would overturn everything we thought we knew about Jane Austen, everything two hundred years of scholarship had labored to teach us about her attitudes, style, and beliefs. I emphasize again, I had nothing to gain, and everything to lose, in thinking the lost sex scenes genuine (though I will add, briefly, that these uncovered pages utilize the same punctuation conventions as her novels—rendering my previous work of some value and *not* obsolete, as the majority of the trend-based scholarship now is without question).

2. For a complete examination of these and other issues, see E. Drummond, "Proof and Prejudice: Authenticating the Lost Austen Erotica," *Journal of Jane Austen Studies,* Vol. 29, No. 6 (2001).

The fact of this book's existence will tell you what I eventually concluded.

How to make sense of the Lost Sex Scenes? I confess here it is beyond my ability. Though this has been the most widely (indeed hysterically) publicized and successful episode in my professional life, it has also been the most disturbing. The new scenes make necessary completely new interpretations of every Austen novel. I suspect it will take decades, and generations of scholars, before their impact is fully absorbed. Until then, the most one can do is present the scenes to the public, in all their original and shocking eroticism. The public, indeed, *must* have their turn. For Austen is not merely a scholarly phenomenon, but a popular one. Her books have been among the most widely read in all of English literature; the new material can only make them more so.

Toward that worthy end, here are the Lost Sex Scenes of Jane Austen.

Elfrida Drummond, Ph.D.
Oxford, England

Pride &

Prejudice

The Letters

The startling material from Jane Austen's most famous work is best introduced by Austen herself. In the first of her rediscovered letters below, she protests, with characteristic directness, her publisher's demand to cut her new novel.

Next, her letter to her sister, Cassandra, elaborates on the censorship episode. It makes clearer yet Austen's determination to explore her characters' sexual lives, and her total lack of embarrassment on the subject.

To Thomas Egerton
Jan 15 [1811]

Sir—

To the many alterations you demand I make to my novel, Pride and Prejudice *(as you would like it called), I must ask one other—which I state below—for you have lopt and cropt so successfully, and in such very sensitive places in the ms., that the book now jumps and meanders over and around the* most important passages—*and I can but wonder what readers will make of the result. My meanings are in some places entirely lost. I see it is in vain that I have laboured to make the little bit of ivory (two inches wide) on which I work with so fine a brush, just a little bit bigger.*

You say the book is indecent. You say I am immodest. But Sir in the depiction of love, modesty is the fullness of truth; *and decency frankness; and so I must also be frank with you, and ask that you remove my name from the title page in all future printings; 'A lady' will do well enough.*

    I remain, dear sir,
      Your obliged and faithl. Hum. serv.
        Jane Austen

Chawton Tuesday January 16 [1811]

My dear Cassandra,
    I am very much obliged to you for all your kind

praise of P&P especially after receiving the most unsettling of letters from JSC. It appears he has taken offence with what he describes as the indecent & immodest aspects of the novel & has asked me to crop out the scenes of love between Elizabeth and Darcy & (this you will not believe) Charlotte and Mr. Collins! He has also made preliminary comments about the trifle with Jane at Netherfield & I am sure it is the next to go. To wit, he added a post-script asking me to change the title from Pride & Promiscuity to Pride & Prejudice. Silly, silly man.

I must confess my surprise & utter disappointment at these thoroughly unpleasant requests. Is he so blind as not to see how very natural are the sorts of displays I detail? I am in desperate need of your counsel & yet I fear that I may have already drop'd all chances of publication. I am ashamed to say I wrote a terribly unladylike letter to JSC stating my thoughts on his suggestions, a copy of which I am enclosing for your perusal (paper is scarce, thus I have copied it on the backside of one of Henry's letters—that men do not use every inch of paper is certainly to be held against them!). You are sure to think less of me when you

see that I asked him to remove my name from the
title page. He will certainly believe me to be the
most unlearned & unmannered female in our
land. . . .

Tuesday. This day's post has just arrived. Frank, of
all people, has written me several lines stating his
highest approbation of the aforementioned scene with
Mr. & Mrs. C! As this was the only scene in the book
he chose to comment on, I am thus all the more
inclined to not oblige JSC with a cruelly reduced
work. Truly, I am feeling the most intolerable anxiety.
I am the first to admit that my novel is but a speck
that only a few limited souls like myself would take
the time to read. However, it is certainly my duty to
make the most of my small talents & I do believe the
novel will be a pale shadow of its former self without
including the simple and everyday sort of diversions
lovers enjoy. Call me in a fit, but I secretly wonder if
JSC knows nothing of these matters. I rather sense
that he & Mrs. C are forever sentenced to their own
bedrooms—it is a little miracle they count 5
children. I know you think me severe & despise me as
the most ungracious ungovernable soul alive. I am
enough alone to know my insufferability. But it is my

unhappy fate to forever disappoint & astonish those I hold most dear! Do not be cross as my impertinence wears thin & I return to my civil & reasonable self more quickly than you might suspect. I shall be extremely impatient to hear your thoughts on these matters. . . .

Your very affecte. Sister
J. Austen

. . . I think we can pronounce you entirely unfit for marriage to our brother.

Jane at Netherfield

This extraordinary section provides a good introduction to the tone and nature of the "lost" material as a whole.

Both scholars and ordinary readers of *Pride and Prejudice* have long been puzzled by the mysterious "Jane's illness" episode. Early in Chapter 7, Jane Bennet is summoned to Netherfield by an urgent letter from Mr. Bingley's sisters ("Come as soon as you can"). Jane does not return home, and the next morning, Elizabeth receives a letter from Jane: "I find myself very unwell this morning . . . my kind friends will not hear of my returning home till I am better."

Most students of the book assume the whole episode is simply a device for luring Elizabeth to Netherfield. But if so, what accounts for the bizarre urgency of the Bingley sisters' invitation? How could Jane in only a few hours become so sick that she can't manage the three-mile trip home to Longbourne? And, most important, how can we explain the complete shift over the course of the novel in the Bingley sisters' attitude toward Jane? The missing section answers these questions, and more.

. . . Jane's day at Netherfield had passed most enjoyably; and, feeling herself by the close of the evening tired indeed, she begged the indulgence of her hosts to be permitted to retire early. Upon receiving their kindest wishes for a good night's rest, she found herself alone in the comfortable bedroom that had been appointed for her, and was soon, and gratefully, asleep.

Jane could not conceive the time of night; indeed, could scarcely recollect where she was, when, to her great alarm, she awoke to find the door to her bedroom being slowly opened.

'Who is there?' she cried.

'Be not alarmed, Miss Bennet, it is only Mrs. Hurst and myself, come to determine that you have been made comfortable.' The voice was that of Miss Caroline Bingley.

'Indeed I have, most comfortable,' replied Jane, 'and I thank you for your kindness.'

The door closed, leaving the room again entirely dark; and Jane was moved at the unexpected demonstration of concern on the part of her visitors, though she wondered at the timing of this particular charitable mission.

'Are you cold, Miss Bennet?' The voice was again Miss Bingley's. They were still in the room! This was most unusual!

'I was, at first,' Jane replied, 'but now I find the extra bed-clothes you provided most marvelously warming. I thank you again for your kind consideration.'

No answer came; and as the room was yet entirely dark Jane could not determine that her assurances had had the intended result, which was to hasten an end to the peculiar conversation.

'What, these bed-clothes?' Now it was Mrs. Hurst's voice! 'These coverings are most thin and threadbare! Miss Bennet, I cannot wonder that you still feel cold.'

'I assure you,' Jane said, 'I do not,' but her speech was interrupted; as, to her almost limitless surprise and shock, she perceived the two sisters, Miss Bingley and Mrs. Hurst, crawl beneath the bed-clothes and arrange themselves therein next to Jane!

'There, Miss Bennet,' said Mrs. Hurst.

'That is much better.'

A moment passed while Jane considered what the best course of action must be.

'Miss Bennet,' said the voice of Miss Bingley, 'no doubt you cannot help but wonder as to the purpose of our visit to you here to-night.'

'Indeed,' replied Jane carefully, 'I have; for though I am most honoured by the attention you have shown me on my visit here at Netherfield, and, truly, have never known greater generosity on the part of any hostess; yet I cannot recollect a time when the attentions of new friends have extended so persistently into the later hours of the night.'

'Allow me to set your mind at ease, Miss Bennet. It cannot have escaped your notice that our brother, Mr. Bingley, favours you exceedingly; and indeed may soon make you a proposal of marriage. No, no, do not protest; for his feelings are plain for all to see. Miss Bennet, our brother is a most unaffectedly modest man, easily guided. You seem a genial, pretty sort of girl; but there are, Miss Bennet, propensities and proclivities, which (and I trust you understand me) do not always become apparent until after marriage; and, as our brother, owing to his modest and unassuming nature, is unlikely to endeavour to make certain inquiries himself, Mrs. Hurst and I have taken it upon ourselves to satisfy our chief concern, namely, that *you* will be able to satisfy *him.*'

Jane, now feeling all the awkwardness and confusion of the situation in which she found herself, immediately, though not very coherently, gave Miss Bingley to understand her objections to the plan now set before her. Her hostess, however, seemed little moved by Jane's arguments; for she, even as Jane continued to speak, was rapidly, and, aided by the skillful hands of Mrs. Hurst, easily divesting Jane of the modest garments which it was her habit to wear a-bed.

Now finding herself quite nude, Jane was most seriously vexed.

'Miss Bennet.' It was the voice of Mrs. Hurst. 'You must chuse, whether to forego forever the affections of our brother; or whether to submit, with what degree of pleasure you may perhaps not now be capable of anticipating, to the investigations of Miss Bingley and myself. The interview will last about one hour. I trust it shall pass quickly.'

The sisters were now themselves entirely unclothed, though Jane could not say, when this transformation had occurred. The three of them lay close together in the bed. Jane was now determined that the time had come to end this matter decisively, and so resolved to speak, directly and with some warmth, on the subject at hand; when she perceived a different sort of warmth, arising from a location on her body below, and from a different sort of hand; the hand, it seemed, of Miss Bingley—or was it Mrs. Hurst? Or both? Jane could not say. She could not speak. It seemed a multitude of hands, and mouths, and lips, and tongues, were now employed at various busy tasks about her body.

The sensation was not entirely unpleasant.

It is the duty of a guest, Jane had always believed, to participate, with enthusiasm if possible, in any games, outings, charades, dances, or other entertainments contrived by the masters of the house where one was staying. And so manners demanded that Jane fully engage in the sometimes languorous, sometimes frenzied, activities devised by the Bingley sisters, whose imagination, endurance, and athletic prowess could only be wondered at.

At one point their introduction of a curiously-shaped carved wooden object into the evening's diversions aroused the most strenuous expressions of concern from Jane; but her objections were quickly silenced by the application of the experienced and skillful hands of Mrs. Hurst.

The hour did pass quickly; and another; and at the close of a third, Ms. Bingley spoke.

'Miss Bennet,' said she, 'you are a most interesting girl. You have surprized us both, I think it safe to say, with your stamina, your extreme pliability, and your eagerness to learn.'

Jane blushed and modestly lowered her eyes.

'Indeed,' said Mrs. Hurst, 'I agree; and I think we can pronounce you entirely unfit for marriage to our brother.'

'Unfit?' Jane cried. 'Unfit? I do not understand.'

'Miss Bennet,' Mrs. Hurst said sharply, 'do you imagine that we could countenance the marriage of our brother to a young woman as wanton, as saucy, as entirely shameless as yourself?'

And with that, Miss Bingley and Mrs. Hurst drew themselves up out of the bed, performed some hasty ablutions with a warm towel, and quit the room.

Tricked! Tricked by the calculations of the Bingley sisters! Jane bitterly rebuked herself for her gullible and trusting nature. It was some hours before she could stop her tears; and some days before she felt well enough to leave her bedroom.

. . . I am rather partial to all things wet, Miss Bennet.
It makes going inside all the more pleasant.

Elizabeth and Darcy

Of perhaps the most celebrated couple in English literature, little more need be said here; volumes have already been devoted to anatomizing Elizabeth Bennet and Fitzwilliam Darcy in all their intricate complexity and charm.

The major issue to be addressed is a simple one. Can a graphic, explicit sex scene between them add anything at all to our understanding of their relationship? Will seeing them, as it were, in action, add to, or merely diminish, the already powerful erotic charge of the courtship so familiar to generations of readers? Austen apparently had her answer; her readers must make of the result what they will.

The restored scene comes halfway through Volume III, Chapter 2; after months of estrangement following Darcy's first, rejected proposal, he and Elizabeth have just had their unexpected meeting at Pemberley.

. . . *They soon outstripped the others, and when they had reached the carriage, Mr. and Mrs. Gardiner were half a quarter of a mile behind.*

He then asked her to walk into the house, but she declared herself not tired, and they stood upon the lawn. At such a time, much might have been said, and silence was very awkward. She wanted to talk, but there seemed an embargo on every subject. *

She looked back, hoping that her Aunt and Uncle's arrival might deliver her; but they had paused a ways off to examine some specimen of flora or fauna, and had come no closer.

Enough, enough of this silence, Elizabeth thought. She would speak. She *must* speak; and having determined to do it, further resolved not to abandon the directness and candour which had characterized all their communications before now.

'Mr. Darcy,' she began. 'It appears we are not to acknowledge all that has passed between us, and are to mark this unexpected meeting only with commonplaces, or, failing that, long silences.'

'If it appears so, Miss Bennet, it is not from

* Italicized text is found in the expurgated, published editions of Austen's novels.

any calculation on my part.'

'Why then have our discussions touched only on fishing, my travels, and the park?'

'These are, I think, reliable subjects, well-known for the unlikelihood of their giving offence,' Mr. Darcy replied. 'On meeting you I resolved to avoid that more troubling species of communication with which we have been acquainted together before.'

'So you are not *entirely* innocent of calculation,' Elizabeth observed.

Mr. Darcy hesitated. 'I admit I am not. Can you say you are?'

'Sir, I cannot,' she replied. They lapsed once more into silence. Elizabeth looked again for her Aunt and Uncle. They were no closer; indeed, had ventured to observe a sheep grazing in a meadow some half a mile distant.

Elizabeth and Darcy were now standing beneath a tree. Mr. Darcy's arm brushed up against Elizabeth's. It was another awkward moment; each stole a glance at the other and muttered apologies in unison as their faces reddened. Elizabeth felt a sudden sense of regret as she looked up to find Mr. Darcy's tender and striking visage, which gazed back upon her. To stem her anxiety, Elizabeth returned to the subject at hand. 'How sad that the intercourse of two such as we should be so dull, not by accident, but by *design* and *calculation*.'

'Perhaps not so sad, Miss Bennet,' Darcy said, continuing to look at her directly. 'We talk too much. We have exhausted ourselves with conversation. Our energies have been dissipated in excess verbosity, our sensibilities sullied by sparring. My own epistolary efforts have worn me out. I am tired, Miss Bennet, and have nothing more of myself to give to weary wit. May we not let our *actions* speak now?'

Darcy raised his hand, meaning, she supposed, to lean against the tree trunk; but instead, to her great surprize, his fingertips moved to her face, where they grazed a tendril of her hair falling outside her cap. Elizabeth looked up to find again Darcy's steadfast gaze; his impenetrable gravity seemed all at once to transform from a natural defect to the most admirable of attributes, and this realisation roused in her the spiritedness he had come to admire.

'So if I take your meaning, sir,' she ventured, 'you are saying, let us dare . . . to be dull?'

He made no immediate answer, but outlined the edge of her muslin frock and slowly dipped his fingertips beneath the fabric. Elizabeth did not move, but closed her eyes and felt the colour again rise to her cheeks. Her face was deeply flushed, and when she opened her eyes, she saw that his was no less so.

'Let us talk, Miss Elizabeth Bennet,' he said, now pressing the length of his body full against hers, '*about the weather.*'

She gasped, and felt a thrill run through her. Elizabeth could hardly conceive that this was the man who only a short time ago seemed the person she most disliked of all her acquaintance!—a man who had ruined the hopes of her dear sister!—a man who had both swelled and diminished her pride in extremes. While her opinion of Mr. Darcy's character had most certainly altered since reading his letter, *this* was a Mr. Darcy she had never before witnessed; a man in some new and puzzling incarnation, so changed, so full of what appeared to be heartfelt play that she scarcely knew how to respond. She stammered and was only able to repeat his own words: 'Talk about the weather?'

Mr. Darcy ran his hand down her cheek as he nodded an assent.

Elizabeth was quick to recover herself and with her full self leaning into him, she returned, 'Very well, sir. How *have* you found the weather to be of late?'

'Very well, thank you.' Now he could barely speak the words.

Both were in the throes of desire; and desire had outstripped sense. Elizabeth took advantage of their weakened state and pulled Mr. Darcy down to the ground. A quick glance over her shoulder confirmed that the Gardiners were deep in conversation with a cow at least a mile off. She arranged him on the grass and with an unexpected gesture sat square on his middle with her muslin gathered round her knees. With leisurely determination she advanced her hands up his chest. She slowed and prolonged the anticipation of their first kiss to a near halt until at last her lips just brushed his.

'I hope the weather has not been too wet for you while at Rosings, Mr. Darcy?' The warm breath of each of Elizabeth's words was felt upon his lips.

'No, I am rather partial to all things wet, Miss Bennet. It makes going inside all the more pleasant.'

Having lain down full-length beside him, Elizabeth soon found him astride *her,* and now, with his mouth pressed hard upon hers, and her lips parted, her tongue was responding to his with alacrity. When the kiss at last broke, their lips were swelled and turned to a deep shade of crimson; and it was she who whispered, 'Do you enjoy cards, Mr. Darcy?' It was the dullest thing she could think of. Both felt a shiver of excitement.

'I am an indifferent card player, Miss Bennet,' he answered, his lips at her neck. 'I value games mostly as an excuse to be near a warm fire.'

'Are you in the habit of running to wherever

a fire is to be had, sir? This sounds quite unlike the hard nature I have been so lucky to observe in you.' Mr. Darcy's hard nature was indeed making itself known most urgently against Elizabeth.

'You are just,' he said as he expertly unbuttoned her frock until her chemise was fully displayed. 'I am often loath to give myself pleasure, with cards or any other object of amusement.' Mr. Darcy put his hands on Elizabeth's breasts and pushed up each soft globe so that both were near escaping the rim of her chemise. Darcy kissed first one, then the other as he reached beneath her undergarments and began to tenderly touch her most sensitive part. Presently it was her excitement that he felt beneath his fingertips. 'And you, Miss Bennett? Are you a game player?' he asked.

'A *tolerable* one, I suppose. But no more,' she replied in a rather lengthy sigh.

She could not help but refer to Mr. Darcy's first impression of her, so many months ago. Darcy pulled away, abashed at the reminder of his previous behaviour.

Clearly her speech could not be trusted to remain unlively. Resolving that her mouth must be put to other uses, Elizabeth dipped her hand into Darcy's breeches and emerged with her prize. Mr. Darcy looked at her with a mix of confusion and gratification.

Darcy closed his eyes as she continued to move her way down to the root of him, employing a natural ease that contradicted her innocence.

Elizabeth was lively in her attentions. By instinct alone, she caressed and licked, bringing Mr. Darcy to the brink of the highest satisfaction. Soon Mr. Darcy was near to his spending and Elizabeth was determined to do what was natural; she sunk her hand between her legs where she remained as she continued to pleasure what appeared to be a thoroughly changed man. Anxious to observe her, Darcy leaned back to obtain a full view of Elizabeth's activities.

And throughout, they continued with several of the most tedious conversations imaginable, covering such subjects as: the price of beeswax candles; preferred horse colours; the various textures of porridge. All the while, Mr. Darcy alternated between embracing and observing Elizabeth as she showed him the activities of her private bedroom, until they were each spent.

Both were very satisfied; and took further satisfaction in the knowledge that throughout, neither had ventured any remark that could be supposed clever by the dullest listener.

They did not speak for some time, and both luxuriated in the pleasant and, to them, unique sensation that nothing at all needed to be said; that the only necessity was to restore the appearance of their clothes, which had been so enthusiastically disturbed.

Presently, though, the Gardiners were perceived in close approach. *At last* it became necessary to once again engage in the most superficial of exchanges. Elizabeth was the first to speak and *recollected that she had been travelling, and they talked of Matlock and Dovedale with great perseverance.*

*The pleasure that each reaped in the giving and
receiving of punishment cannot be underestimated.*

Charlotte and Mr. Collins

If Austen is peerless in her depiction of happy couples like Elizabeth and Darcy, she is no less adept in her portraits of unhappy ones. There is scarcely a worse match in her corpus than that of Charlotte Lucas, Elizabeth's straightforward, impoverished friend, and Mr. Collins—pompous vicar, rejected suitor of Elizabeth, and slave to his patron Lady Catherine de Bourgh. Their marriage is so dismal that readers and critics have often joined Elizabeth herself in wondering how Charlotte could possibly survive it.

As the restored section below makes clear, Austen anticipated this concern, and addressed it in a way previously unimagined.

Mr. Collins was at his usual post in the book-room, awaiting the passing phaeton of Miss de Bourgh or the great honour of a visit from Lady Catherine de Bourgh, herself. The latter was his singular object and he spent hours in wait of any sign of his patroness. Charlotte walked into an adjacent room, where a parcel had just been left for her. To her chagrin, she caught her husband's notice.

'Mrs. Collins! Can you believe our good fortune this morning?'

'Has something happened of which I am not aware?' asked Charlotte.

'Why you are looking directly on it! The parcel—did you not see the parcel that Lady Catherine's footman left for you? I would have notified you immediately, but wanted you to have the full satisfaction of coming onto it yourself.'

'Oh yes, I see it,' she calmly replied.

'I will leave to you the honours of opening it as, I am certain, must be your desire.'

Charlotte, contrary to her husband's assurances, had no particular desire to open the parcel at that moment, as their patroness and frequent visitor made requisite a constant eye on housekeeping and an unending array of chores to complete; yet open the parcel she did, as Mr. Collins would not be satisfied otherwise.

Charlotte untied the wrapping. Inside she

found a gown. Though clearly not new, it was not in bad condition; and indeed, would have been the very height of fashion had the date been some fifteen years earlier. 'How odd,' said Charlotte. 'I wonder what this could be for?'

Mr. Collins regarded his wife with a look of the highest gratification. 'I can scarcely believe the condescension her ladyship has just bestowed on you. I do believe, Mrs. Collins, that this was once Lady Catherine's very own garment—I recall a watercolour in the library in which our patroness' gown is of a distinct resemblance.'

'How very strange of her to give it to me,' Charlotte responded evenly. 'We are far from the same size, and though I am certainly not one to wear the latest styles, it would hardly be to anyone's distinction to have me in this now.'

'I am certain you have only *momentarily* lost your awareness of the compliment being paid to you by the Right Honourable Lady Catherine de Bourgh,' said Mr. Collins, puffed with great solemnity and marked displeasure, 'and I know that you will surely realise anon that to don anything of Lady Catherine's would be a testament of her beneficence if not a great compliment to us both, that our patroness would consider our material comfort so particularly. Few can boast of such attentions, Mrs. Collins; I assure you, *very* few!'

Charlotte said nothing in return, yet felt keenly the unsuitability of her match—as she could not help but feel from time to time. One particular phantasy followed close upon these sentiments, as it and others of an equally violent nature often did. The image of Mr. Collins stepping on the garden rake only to be solidly clocked in the head, never to rise again (a rake he had dropped some time ago along a seldom-used path while in a frenzy to greet Lady Catherine, and which he subsequently forgot to retrieve) gave her comfort and steadied her thoughts. But Charlotte's sensible, steady nature kept her from dwelling on the phantasy. Instead, she made a quiet exit and escaped to the drawing-room, while Mr. Collins persisted in his rapturous praise of his patroness.

Charlotte resumed her housekeeping;

within moments however, she was filled with so keen a delight that she was hardly able to stand. An extraordinary idea, a daring, exquisite notion, had struck her. She gasped for breath. It was in this state that Charlotte unfolded the gown and held it up to her person. That the dress was far too large—Lady Catherine being several inches taller and unquestionably wider—was irrefutable. Charlotte easily slipped the garment over her clothing with still more room to spare. She then filled out the bust with two rags she was to use to polish the silver.

She now changed her posture, her voice, and the look upon her face in imitation of the one who had once inhabited the gown. 'Mr. & Mrs. Collins!,' she said. 'What is this rubbish I see lying upon the table here? Housekeeping should be the uppermost priority in a domestic arrangement such as yours where a servant cannot be on hand for every whim. Carelessness is a crime and I do not tolerate any form of it. ——Even at Rosings, I am excessively attentive to all such details. It is often wondered at, how I can do so much with so little time, and yet, I manage splendidly, Mrs. Collins; hence *you*—with your *very few* responsibilities—most certainly can.' Though the mime was imperfect, the words were an exact study of Lady Catherine's lexicon. The speech could have come directly from Lady Catherine, herself.

'Are you speaking to me, Mrs. Collins?' Charlotte heard from the dining-room.

'No, Mr. Collins. I was merely composing my thank-you to Lady Catherine,' Charlotte replied.

'Very good, Mrs. Collins. You are right to do so.'

Charlotte smiled complacently and moved —as if in response to the real Lady Catherine—to snap up the paper and string used to tie up the parcel. On doing so, she was surprised to find another object still inside the packaging. Charlotte reached her hand in and pulled out a riding crop. It was old and bruised, and bits of leather had worn loose from excessive use.

Charlotte examined the crop and slapped her leg with it, only to let out a little cry on realising how effective it remained. Her liveliness increased with her new discovery and Charlotte continued with her mime. 'Mr. Collins, you must find a way to improve the peonies out front. A peony that leans is one that is not to be permitted! I am very disappointed in you, Mr. Collins.'

Charlotte heard shuffling from the other room, 'Mrs. Collins! Mrs. Collins! I do not know how, but I believe Lady Catherine is here.'

'Mr. Collins, I am in the drawing-room,' she scolded, in imitation of Lady Catherine.

Mr. Collins entered the drawing-room near breathless, explaining—'Lady Catherine, my most earnest apologies, I do not know how it is possible, but I did not hear—' He stopt suddenly as his eye beheld, not Lady Catherine, but his own lady standing in a manner most entirely unknown to him and yet wholly familiar; for the first time in the whole course of his life, Mr. Collins was unable to speak.

'Mr. Collins, if I am to pay you a visit, I certainly expect to be greeted at the door. If I can stroll in without anyone's notice, I can only assume the same to be the case for any unknown passer-by. This is not the sort of behaviour I expect from one in my employ, Mr. Collins. I will have you know that without question.'

Mr. Collins continued to look at his wife in awe. His mouth stood agape. At last he said tentatively, 'I will not flatter myself with your forgiveness. No, I have been very, very remiss.'

'That is putting it mildly, Mr. Collins. I am only an occasional advocate of severe punishment, yet I believe one must learn that there are consequences to one's actions.'

Words were insufficient to express the astonishment *and* satisfaction Mr. Collins felt at this very new sort of attention from one, in words, indistinguishable from Lady Catherine de Bourgh.

'Mr. Collins, I always speak my mind and I will not hesitate now. One such as you must learn from your mistakes the hard way. Position yourself, at once, on your hands and knees.—Any hesitation will most certainly result in a more painful consequence.' Charlotte's last words were unnecessary; Mr. Collins had thrown himself at her feet before her speech was completed.

'Are you prepared to suffer for your stupidity and inadequacy as a husband, cleric, and Englishman?' Charlotte asked with indignation.

Mr. Collins whimpered a quiet assent.

'Respond aloud when spoken to,' Charlotte commanded.

Mr. Collins lowered his body down flat to the floor in a solemn bow and said, in a confusion of thanks and apologies, 'Permit me to beg pardon, Your Ladyship. You invariably know the inevitable excitement of your excessively generous attentions of which I in no manner expected to receive in this form today.'

'Enough long speeches, Mr. Collins; one of your shocking failures is your inability to understand that your inferior rank demands more listening and less chatter—a lesson you have hardly learned and one which I, in my extraordinary kindness, have not made a determined point of.'

Yet, Mr. Collins' obsequious manner could not be contained; speak he must. He began to nod and apologise until Charlotte brusquely cut him off, 'Mr. Collins, you lie on the floor like a lame dog without its wits—waiting to praise any punishment you receive.'

'It can only be called an honour to be your dog, Lady Catherine,' said Mr. Collins.

'A dog allowed to remain in the house must obey every command. If you want not to be put out, go fetch that crop on the ottoman.'

Mr. Collins went to stand, but Charlotte would have none of it. Mr. Collins was to fetch on all fours and to retrieve with his mouth, providing a momentary respite to his verbal excesses. Mr. Collins looked to be in near violent ecstasy as he trotted to the ottoman, let out a bark, and grabbed the crop with his teeth. Charlotte, herself, felt a keen rush of pleasure quite unlike anything she had known before.

'A dog must accept any punishment he is given, but a *man* has the power to conceive of his own punishment—and then, if he has any tenacity, to ask for more. What are you, Mr. Collins? Are you a *man* or a *dog?*'

The question left Mr. Collins in a state of

confusion, not so much due to a lack of understanding, but to an inability to decide which
answer was the one his Ladyship most wanted
to hear. Mr. Collins attempted a response, but
was stopped by the crack of the whip against his
backside. For a few solitary moments, as the
sensation of stinging and burning was most felt,
silence ensued. Each party entered their own
private rhapsody, never to be matched with such
intensity again. Each felt their power or power-
lessness (as was appropriate) rise to unaccountable heights. And each felt a resulting quiver
and a warmth so penetrating that their breath
raced in unison.

'I have been very, very bad! May I please
have another!', poured from his lips, along with
a series of barks and growls.

With each request for further punishment,
Charlotte bore down all the more mercilessly
upon his flesh until both came to a sort of cli-
max neither had ever observed in the other, and
quite possibly had never experienced unto
themselves.

The pleasure that each reaped in the giving

and receiving of punishment cannot be underestimated. The number of lashings, the specific
feelings aroused, and the effect of this turn of
events on the future of each party will not be
elaborated upon here. Suffice it to say that, on
the whole, there was a justice born of Charlotte's spirited actions that allowed her to live a
life less checked and more tolerable than might
have been surmised otherwise.

Sense & Sensibility

And so I reached down and put my hand on top of it!
On what?
It!

Such Devoted Sisters

The two sisters at the heart of *Sense and Sensibility*, Elinor and Marianne Dashwood, are polar opposites in their approach to romantic experience. Elinor, the older sister, has a long, tentative, often-frustrated courtship with the reticent Edward Ferrars; Marianne plunges headlong into a torrid romance with the Byronic Mr. Willoughby. Throughout the book, much is said about the tensions arising between the Misses Dashwood from their very different temperaments— but much is left unsaid too. From the missing section, it is clear that Austen originally intended a much more specific (and realistic) depiction of sisterly conversation.

'Elinor,' cried Marianne, 'is this fair? Is this just? Are my ideas so scanty? But I see what you mean. I have been too much at my ease, too happy, too frank. I have erred against every commonplace notion of decorum; I have been open and sincere where I ought to have been reserved, spiritless, dull, and deceitful:

had I talked only of the weather and the roads, and had I spoken only once in ten minutes this reproach would have been spared.'

Their mother retreated to another room; her nerves did not allow for discord. As soon as she left, Marianne continued, 'And yet, in truth you have heard and seen so little—you know nothing of what goes on between Willoughby and me when we steal a few moments together, away from all the incessant monotony of our everyday lives. Are you not aching to know what we speak of when we truly speak our minds?'

'I believe,' Elinor replied, 'that I can live without that knowledge.'

Marianne, who did not mean to provoke her sister, saw that her approach had been wrong, and she now adopted a more playful tone. 'My dearest sister, it is only that I wish us to be true *confidantes,* with no secrets between us. Let it be a proper exchange, then. I shall tell all about Willoughby and you shall tell me of Edward. Yes, Edward, for I know well that much must have transpired between you— much that is secret and thrilling and—' Here speech failed her and she burst into an excited shriek. 'Oh tell me, please, Elinor, tell me!'

It was Elinor's habit of long standing to humour her sister; and though her sense of propriety was too strong to be abandoned completely, she felt that some concession to sisterly intimacy was now hers to make. She loved Marianne too dearly to thwart an open and honest moment between them. And, she confessed to herself, her curiosity was aroused. 'Of Edward and myself, I profess there is nothing to say,' Elinor began. 'However, my untamed sister who detests all things dull and deceitful, if you *were* to tell me something of Willoughby, I suppose I would not quit the room.'

'Oh! That is my true heart! You are so good and now I shall entertain you with many, many secrets!' Marianne cried.

'As always, the younger Miss Dashwood is given an inch and she takes a mile. Be gentle with me, Marianne, you know how modest I am.'

'Or claim to be. We shall see how modest you truly are when your turn comes.'

Elinor did not remember saying anything

about her turn, but she stifled this objection, as Mrs. Dashwood had appeared. Their mother pretended to look for her needlework for a moment; then, satisfied that all was well between her girls, she left the room.

'I shall now tell you of our first meeting, as you only know the half of it.'

Elinor was surprised; she could not imagine what had been left uncovered, as Marianne had told the story again and again in great detail. Now she began it once more. 'As you know, I fell, and before I could call out, Willoughby approached. In the fall, my frock was every place but where it was meant to be, and when Willoughby leant down to lift me, I noticed, to my great distress, that my bosom was almost fully exposed.'

Elinor gasped.

'I blushed and averted my eyes, but Willoughby did not let me grieve. He said without hesitation, "What a glorious day, Miss. So many of nature's beauties to feast one's eyes upon," and then he smiled and lifted me up without allowing me to put myself back together.'

Elinor shrieked, half in glee, half in horror. Mrs. Dashwood ran in upon hearing such a sound, only to be assured that nothing was amiss. When their mother had gone again, Elinor spoke. 'Marianne, it cannot be so! Oh! I think I could not have kept my composure. What did you say? How did you gain your wits?'

'I think I did not. Nor have I yet!' Marianne exclaimed. 'I simply replied, "If only what I felt at this very moment could also be gazed upon, I am quite sure I would know true satisfaction." To which he replied, "And what feeling is pressed upon you? Can you put your finger on it—the exact nature of this feeling?" And so I reached down and put my hand on top of it!'

'On what?'

'It!'

'You did not!'

'I did so!'

'It?'

'Yes, it!'

It was a moment before Elinor could speak. 'How could you? Where was your modesty, Marianne?'

'And when have I ever been modest? You are thinking only of yourself, Elinor. Remember, I know nothing of decorum or reserve. Besides, it is not as if he had no breeches on! Now it is your turn.'

Elinor sat gazing at her sister disapprovingly, or so Marianne believed. That much had passed between Marianne and Elinor in their lives thus far was indisputable, but Elinor's reserve had always prevented the kind of discussion that other, less guarded, sisters enjoyed.

'Oh, don't look so dismayed, Elinor!' Marianne cried. ''Tis only love!—Not murder!'

'I am speechless. That is all. I do not know how to craft my response.'

'And why must a response be crafted? Speak from your heart. Leave off your self-command and conceal nothing! And if you do not, then I shall draw it out of you little by little.' Without waiting to hear if a response was imminent, Marianne at once drew close to her sister and whispered, 'Now you and Edward. Have you held hands? I know you have! I am sure. Tell me where and when?'

Elinor blushed again.

Marianne eagerly awaited her sister's reply. When none came, her impatience and imagination took command. 'It must have been the last time we were at John's. We all went for a walk and you and Edward strayed off the path to give his broken-down old stallion an apple.'

'Broken-down, Marianne? I think it is a very handsome beast—gentle, fleet of foot, firm of flank.'

''Tis not the point, Elinor,' replied Marianne, irritated that her phantasy had been interrupted. 'Yes, you two went off and Fanny was in a state of anxiety—I am sure because she thought Edward was proposing. Am I right, Elinor? I know you shall confirm my suspicion.'

Elinor was silent.

'You are not fun at all!' Marianne admonished. 'Why must I draw you out? Am I not your own sister? Have I not revealed the greatest intimacies to you?'

'Please forgive me, Marianne. I do not mean to appear cold-hearted. I am cautious—too cautious, I am sure.' Elinor's response roused her sister to greater affection; Marianne did not like to see Elinor suffer.

'You silly goose. We are just playing. Do not be hard on yourself. Your spirits have been dampened and now I am going to cheer you with more stories of romance and passion. I shall tell you of the little notes Willoughby passes me when no one is looking—"Marianne, your lips, filled with every rosy blossom, tempt me to great madness."' Marianne had adopted the grave, dulcet tones that she always used for recitation. Before she could go on, Elinor interrupted.

'Stop!' she cried. 'I will tell you about Edward. At least then I shall not be forced to hear another word of Willoughby's preposterously silly verse.'

Marianne was piqued for but an instant by Elinor's remark; her curiosity as to what Elinor would say far outweighed her irritation. She pressed her sister to continue. And, at last, Elinor spoke; and her confession occupied some twenty minutes by the clock.

When she finished, it was Marianne who

could not speak. It could not be! Edward's beloved dappled stallion *and* Edward himself? Was it possible? Not with *her* Elinor! Nay, with anyone! Marianne could not believe what she had heard. Not even her wildest imaginings had predicted the astonishing communication that Elinor, in all her customary steady composure, had related to her sister. Astounded and gleeful, Marianne cried, 'And *you* chastised *me* about my behaviour with Willoughby! Is that fair? Compared to *you,* it is as if I only spoke of the weather or the roads!' And here again, out of her sheer delight in her dear sister's outraged propriety, she shrieked loudly, and with abandon. The sound promptly brought Mrs. Dashwood into the room again, in a state of great agitation and concern; and it was some time before the two sisters could convince their mother that nothing, truly, was amiss.

. . . Mr. Palmer folded his newspaper, put himself to bed, and with hardly a grunt fell asleep.

The Palmers

Once again, playing on the theme of the ill-matched couple, Jane Austen presents us with the Palmers. The too happy daughter of Mrs. Jennings and her dour husband may be secondary characters, but they are primary examples of marriage gone awry. Elinor herself wonders at "the strange unsuitableness which often existed between husband and wife." And later decides, "His temper might perhaps be a little soured by finding, like many another of his sex, that through some unaccountable bias in favor of beauty, he was the husband of a very silly woman. . . ." The Palmers serve as a warning to Elinor and particularly to Marianne, a warning to make no marital decision in haste, for the results are all too devastatingly clear, as displayed in the following missing scene.

The evening passed steadily; tea had been served, the card table put away, and near everyone had gone to bed, including Mr. Palmer.

Only Mrs. Palmer and her mother remained until, at last, Mrs. Jennings put an end to the conversation.——And this she did only to insure her being the first one up; for it was antithetical to her nature to miss activity of any kind. Consequently, Mrs. Palmer was left no one with whom to extend her good humour and happy nature.

Cleveland had its first moment of quiet since the day began. Mrs. Palmer *did* have several hearty laughs as she recollected earlier conversations, but these moments were interrupted by silence; even Mrs. Palmer was unable, on her own, to keep a steady stream of noise. Once she had fussed with everything that could be fussed with, she went upstairs to her dressing-room where she changed into her new set of bedding clothes. These she dampened to show off her well-rounded figure and made her way to her chamber.

Before the door was fully ajar, Mrs. Palmer announced herself to her husband (who was shielded by his habitual newspaper) with a wealth of good cheer. 'It is only I, love! Why who else could it be? How silly of me!——I do hope I didn't startle you, my love. I would have been up sooner, but Mama and I were having the exceedingly best of conversations. But I am monstrously sorry to have kept you waiting.'

No response was made to his wife's concerns.

'Are you awake, my love? Would not that be something if I was talking and asking you questions when you were asleep! Of course it would not be the first time!' Mrs. Palmer enjoyed this thought immensely and continued to laugh until she interrupted herself, 'Now, my love, I cannot wait for you to slyly comment on my new bedding clothes. You know how impatient I am—I think it will kill me to wait for you to come up with one of your witty quips. Do look, my love, and tell me what you think.'

'A stunning example of unnecessary expense wed to lower-class sensibility, or should I say insensibility,' was his reply.

'How droll you are, love! I must remember to tell the Misses Dashwood your remark,' Mrs. Palmer said, laughing heartily.

'If you do, you will only show yourself to be a ridiculous fool.'

Mrs. Palmer seemed not to hear her husband's remonstrance—it rather appeared to spur her to continue. 'I am sure Miss Marianne's spirits will be lifted when I quote you. How delighted she shall be! It is just the thing to help her through her heartbreak. Morning can't come soon enough.—Now, my luscious plum, do I have a treat for you! Close your eyes!'

Whether her luscious plum's eyes actually closed, one will never know. Mr. Palmer was perfectly invisible to his wife—his newspaper covering everything from his waist up. Mrs. Palmer, nonetheless, acted swiftly so as not to keep Mr. Palmer waiting; or, perhaps, she was simply eager to show off her surprise. In little time, she stood fully exposed save a camisole with two perfectly placed openings and a cap of purple feathers to match.

'You may open your eyes, my sweet! Is it not astonishing?—modelled after a French costume, I was told. Mrs. Tulliver had it made for me. She knows a dressmaker who is next to a milliner and the two do all sorts of monstrous naughty pieces, my love. Can you imagine Mrs.

Tulliver? But 'tis true! I do swear it! She was kind enough to place the order for me. You can imagine my embarrassment at ordering such a garment. I told her, only for my Mr. Palmer would I do such a thing! Of course I am all delight. You cannot believe how many times your reaction has raced through my mind, my love. I was given goose bumps with each new thought.'

Mrs. Palmer went on to acquaint her husband with all her many phantasies. She talked of scenarios: Mr. Palmer as a gypsy who comes to attack her along the solitary road to the village; Mr. Palmer as a Vicar who loves to dole out *all sorts* of advice to his parishioners; and even some notion related to Mr. Palmer, Mrs. Palmer, and a bellows—a notion rather too indelicate to repeat. And yet, silence continued to be the only response from her better half.

It was Mrs. Palmer's unique character that enabled her to sustain a conversation whether the party she addressed chose to join in or not. And, most surprisingly, she was able to do so with perfect joy. The lack of encouragement she received from her husband seemed merely to furnish her with an extra enthusiasm.

'Now, my love, tell me what you would like me to do.'

'Go to bed,' was his only answer.

'You are so droll! In truth, my sweetness. I will do anything you ask. Or I will play the innocent and you may do anything you like to me. Yes, make me the virgin. I am your young, virgin half-sister whom you have never met!'

'I have no half-sister.'

'It is all play, love. We shall pretend that you do.'

'I cannot imagine anything as imbecilic. Go to bed, Charlotte.'

'Oh! You want me in bed so you can sneak up on me! Very clever, love! Are you going to play the naughty footman? Or the butler? Yes, the butler, love. Do play the butler! I shall pretend to be asleep, but I shall leave the covers off—as if I'd kicked them in the night! Then you may come and do what you will with me and I shall shriek and then fall into a great passion with you!'

'The devil! What is this putrid odor emanating from my candle? Charlotte, is this not beeswax?'

'No, it is a tallow, love. I thought you would be proud of me for thinking of expense. We saved a bundle, love. I know you would not expect me to be so conscientious, but—'

'Are you mad? And why did you not consult me?' he said with great disdain.

'Love, it is nothing that cannot be changed tomorrow.—In the meantime, my sweet pudding, I can think of something for you to do with what is left of that delightful taper!' Mrs. Palmer raised her brow.

On that, Mr. Palmer folded his newspaper, put himself to bed, and with hardly a grunt fell asleep.

'What a temper! Yet, I do love it! He is all sweetness at his core.—Hardly a woman as lucky as I exists! Yes, I am quite convinced there can be no one happier!' Mrs. Palmer continued in good cheer. She smiled, smiled some more and allowed no interruption to her gaiety, despite the fact she was left alone to explore her fancies. And it was not until Mrs. Palmer fell into a deep sleep that her smile disappeared entirely from her face.

Mansfield Park

. . . having abandoned his scruples in regard to the play itself, he was now willing to abandon everything else, including his trousers.

The Play

"You are not serious, Tom, in meaning to act? . . . I think it would be very wrong."

Thus Edmund Bertram's opening volley against the controversial project at the heart of *Mansfield Park:* the production of a play. With Sir Thomas Bertram away from home, the thrill-seeking Tom, Maria, and Julia Bertram—along with Maria's fiancé, Mr. Rushworth, and the flirtatious brother-sister team of Henry and Mary Crawford—line up in favor of the scheme. On the anti side are the righteous cousins, Henry Bertram and Fanny Price.

Why are Henry and Fanny so opposed to what seems like a harmless entertainment? And why should the selected play, the innocuous *Lovers' Vows,* scandalize them so? Their extreme opposition has led modern readers of the book to classify them as boring, humorless prigs, and Sir Thomas—who upon arriving home orders the production halted and the stage destroyed—as a tyrant.

As the restored section below demonstrates, however, *Lovers' Vows* was not Austen's original choice of material; and Edmund and Fanny were right to be shocked.

~~~~~~~~~~~~~~~~~~~~~~~~~~~~~~~~~~~~~~~

The business of finding a play that would suit everybody proved to be no trifle; and the carpenter had received his orders and taken his measurements, had suggested and removed at least two sets of difficulties, and having made the necessity of an enlargement of plan and expense baldly evident, was already at work, while a play was still to seek. Other preparations were also in hand. An enormous roll of green baize had arrived from Northampton, and had been cut out by Mrs. Norris (with a saving, by her good management, of full three quarters of a yard) and was actually forming into a curtain by the handmaids, and still the play was wanting and as two or three days passed away in this manner, Edmund began almost to hope that none might even be found.

Maria had made the first proposal; of a play she had heard of being put on by friends the previous summer, with great results, called *The Curious Cousins*. Upon reading the work (credited only to 'An Energetic Gentleman'), Edmund could not for several hours bring himself to speak.

Later, however, when he was alone with his sister, he took the opportunity of saying, 'I could not, before the others, speak what I feel as to this play, without reflecting on people of their acquaintance, but now I must ask you, is this the sort of entertainment nowadays put on publicly, without shame, in respectable homes?' Maria hastened to assure him that it was not; but indeed, only privately, and late at night, and rarely even then; but only in the company of one's dearest and most trusted and most intimate friends, and were not the Crawfords and Mr. Rushworth these? And, she went on, this particular play was not chosen idly, but only after considering and discarding many others, which she then named.

Edmund was unfamiliar with them. He had not read, or even heard of, *The Saucy Footman, The Peculiar Education of Lady G., The Vigorous Vicar,* or *A Most Distressingly Bumpy Barouche;* but he felt certain the fault lay not with his education, but with her selections, the titles of which he could scarcely contemplate without colouring.

'I must tell you,' Edward said, 'that I find *The Curious Cousins* exceedingly unfit for private representation; and I hope that you will give it up. Read only the first scene aloud, to either your mother or aunt, and see how you can approve it.—It will not be necessary to send you to your father's judgement, I am convinced."

'We see things very differently,' cried Maria. 'I am perfectly acquainted with the play, I assure you. It will be performed after Mother and our Aunt and the servants have gone to bed; and with a very few omissions, and so forth, which will be made, of course, I can see nothing objectionable in it.'

'I assume you are speaking of the pic-nic scene, as one you intend to omit.'

'The pic-nic scene!' cried Maria. 'To the contrary, the pic-nic scene is essential, and charming besides; without it, the viewer should never learn of the cousins' great delight in nature.'

'In nature?' replied Edward. 'But what occurs is entirely unnatural and, I think (from what little knowledge I have derived from extensive study of classical sculpture) anatomically implausible. This pic-nic is like no pic-nic I have ever been on, or heard described. Does not one embark on such an outing with the aim of enjoying a meal in an Arcadian setting? Yet the consumption of food here is entirely secondary to their purpose.'

'Edmund, the curious cousins eat later, after they have returned to the house and bathed. You cannot have us omit the scene. We have had an entire back-drop painted.'

'But my sister,' cried Edmund, now gone quite grey in his agitation, 'do you really propose to *do* all that the play calls for? It is quite impossible.'

'Impossible, yes; it is impossible too that an actor in the role of Hamlet die each night falling on Laertes' sword. Of course he does not die; it is contrived for the stage; it is acting.'

'I comprehend. So in the play,' said Edmund, stammering, 'Mimsy and Yvonne will not, I mean to say that they will not actually, that is . . . fall upon Bernard's . . . sword?'

'That is for Tom to determine; he is staging the production.'

Edmund immediately quit the room and contrived to speak privately with his brother. With some warmth, he made plain his objections, both on the grounds of decency and with regard to the difficulties in stage-craft involved. By concluding with a sincerely-felt assessment of the potential for actual physical danger on the part of the female performers, owing to the lack of costuming and the chilly conditions of the theater, he had nearly persuaded his brother to give up the notion. 'Let us at least avoid subjecting our sisters and Miss Crawford to draughts, Tom.'

'Perform a play with no women?' said Tom. 'Where would we find such a play?'

'I fear it would be difficult,' replied Edmund in a hopeful tone.

'Wait a moment. I do recall something, merely a trifle, a sort of humorous jape performed by Navy-men at sea. I have heard sailors speak of it with great affection. It is called *The Three Lonesome Deck-Hands; or, A Romance of the West Indies*. Perhaps Fanny's brother could aid us in finding a copy—he is at sea, is he not? We would have to repaint the back-drop. . . .'

But this plan soon proved impractical, and, with Mr. Crawford and Mr. Rushworth emphatically declining roles, it was abandoned. *The Curious Cousins* was taken up again.

[Some chapters later, as is familiar to readers of the expurgated version, the play is about to be rehearsed, with both Edmund and Fanny having reluctantly taken roles.]

The first regular rehearsal of the first three acts was certainly to take place in the evening; and every one concerned was looking forward with eagerness.

But Fanny still hung back. She could not endure the idea of it. After much entreaty she had agreed, with sinking heart, to take the role of Yvonne, the French ladies' maid; and now stood trembling and miserable in the costume that had been prepared for her. She detested the costume. Mary Crawford, who claimed to know of such things, insisted it was delightfully true to the modern French fashion, and becoming to Fanny besides; but Fanny could not help but think that—true to the French fashion indeed!—it was both painfully constricting and altogether shameless at once; and, her arm growing weary under the weight of the pic-nic basket she was to carry in the scene, she anticipated her entrance with dread.

She was to enter upon the conclusion of a scene between Edmund and Miss Crawford—or rather, 'Bernard' and 'Mimsy.' Edmund, whose fulminations against the performance had been even more vociferous than her own, was now, she was surprized to see, acquitting himself admirably in the role.

As 'Bernard' (described only as 'A Well-Formed Fellow' by the play-text), Edmund wore a velvet cloak; a three-cornered hat in the continental style; and a pair of high, sturdy hunting boots borrowed from Tom. Fanny had been surprized and dismayed that Edmund did not insist on wearing more, as was his usual habit. It seemed that, having abandoned his scruples in regard to the play itself, he was now willing to abandon everything else, including his trousers. She feared that his capitulation had something to do with his partner in the scene, Mary Crawford, who now stood before him dressed only in the three quarters of a yard of green baize which had been left over from the curtain.

And, Fanny knew, before long even that modest covering would be gone, for the scene called for 'Mimsy' to lay it on the ground upon learning that 'Yvonne' had forgotten the pic-nic cloth. For this error 'Yvonne' was to be, in the words of the script, 'punished most delight-fully.'

Punishment indeed! First to watch her beloved Edmund, in hip boots, flirt and more with the undeniably attractive Miss Crawford; then to be thrust in amongst their amorous exertions herself! Fanny wished most heartily that she were up in her room reading Cowper.

But her entrance was upon her, and she

began her part in the scene.

Soon the baize was on the 'ground'; soon 'Bernard's' cloak and hat were cast away; now the removable panel built into the front of Fanny's uniform had been 'torn off' in a 'rage' by 'Mimsy,' thus causing the uniform to drop to the floor; and there Fanny stood, mute, trembling, exposed in only her underclothes, before Edmund, the cousin whose modesty and rectitude had long been an example to her, but who had now, it seemed, risen most unexpectedly to this peculiar occasion; and Miss Crawford, the friend for whose affections she had often been grateful, but whose motives, especially with regard to Edmund, Fanny had never been able to regard without some suspicion and occasional dismay. All, except Fanny, were now entirely naked. All knew their parts, knew what was to follow in the complicated scene; knew what gestures, what exclamations, what complex and intricate choreography was to come. All knew they must begin.

They did *begin*—*and being too much engaged in their own noise, to be struck by unusual noise in the* other part of the house, had proceeded some way when the door of the room was thrown open, and Julia appearing in it, with a face all aghast, exclaimed, 'My father is come! He is in the hall at the moment!'

I calculate I am exactly eight inches away from you, Fanny.

Henry and Mary Crawford

Fanny and Edmund, cousins raised as brother and sister, eventually marry, but not without questions as to the morality of such a match. We are given a glimpse of Fanny's thoughts on the matter and are made to understand just how sensitive the subject is: "To think of him as Miss Crawford might be justified in thinking, would in her be insanity. To her, he could be nothing under any circumstances—nothing dearer than a friend. Why did such an idea occur to her even enough to be reprobated and forbidden? It ought not to have touched on the confines of her imagination."

All the while, the flirtatious, attractive siblings Henry and Mary Crawford continually tempt the heroes: Henry woos Fanny while the seductive Mary comes perilously close to landing Edmund. The incestuous subtext of all of this cross brother-sister romance has been much commented on, especially by modern (and postmodern) critics. But in the recovered scene below, subtext becomes text, and much recent, trendy scholarship is rendered forever obsolete as the question of the limits of love between family members is taken to its extreme.

Henry is addressing Mary as we begin:

'But I cannot be satisfied without Fanny Price, without making a small hole in Fanny Price's heart. . . . She is quite a different creature from what she was in the autumn. She was then merely a quiet, modest, not plain looking girl, but she is now absolutely pretty. I used to think she had neither complexion nor countenance; but in that soft skin of hers, so frequently tinged with a blush as it was yesterday, there is decided beauty; and from what I observed of her eyes and mouth, I do not despair of their being capable of expression enough when she has anything to express. And then——her air, her manner, her tout ensemble is so indescribably improved! She must be grown two inches, at least, since October.'

'Phoo! phoo! This is only because there were no tall women to compare her with, and because she has got a new gown, and you never saw her so well dressed before. She is just what she was in October, believe me. . . . If you do set about a flirtation with her, you never will persuade me that it is in compliment to her beauty, or that it proceeds from anything but your own idleness and folly.'

To this accusation, her brother gave only a lazy sort of smile, and it was some time before he stirred himself enough to say, 'Mary, I believe you are jealous.'

'Hardly, Henry,' his sister replied. 'It is only that your Fanny-rhapsody is tiresome. Rhetorical excesses do you no good service; they only make you seem an unguarded, foolish sort of man. I deplore exaggeration when put to the wrong use.'

'My dear sister, let me again assure you I hold you above all other women in every regard. On *that* subject I could not exaggerate.'

'Do not bait me, Henry. I do not speak from *jealousy*. A sister feels no jealousy for a brother's passing fancy. Let us say no more upon the matter.'

And they did not, not for several long hours, while Henry affected to read a book, and Mary to write dull letters she had no particular inclination to post, in answer to letters she wished had never been posted to *her;* until both agreed that the afternoon's enforced idleness, a result of the weather, had made them irritable and sleepy, and they must take some air or go mad. They would brave the intermittent rains for half an hour. They left the house. They walked; and Henry took up the conversation as if no time had passed:

'My dear, Fanny's figure is *nothing* compared to yours, and her complexion plain when put next to your own.'

'Henry, I cannot believe you did not hear me before. You must stop teazing me at once.'

'Is it teazing, to speak one's true heart?' Henry asked. 'Then you teaze me, dear sister, when you speak of Edward.'

'Edmund.'

'Edward, Edmund, whomever. He is an appalling man. But I will not go on; you love him—or pretend to.'

They said no more, both having sensed that the conversation had strayed again into dangerous and unwelcome territory. Their walk was not refreshing, and after a short time they returned to the house and resumed their former places in the drawing-room.

They found the atmosphere unchanged; it was as dead, as stifling, and altogether maddening a place to be as any either could remember.

Henry took up his book but could not even affect to read. After a very few moments he flung the book away, and strode in an agitated manner twice about the room, before coming to sit next to his sister on the couch.

'Let me teaze no more, Mary,' said Henry. 'You are everything I desire in a woman. You know my views. Fanny is a trifle. I toy with her because I cannot have you.' With this, Henry passed his hand over his sister's hair and removed a pin holding one of her curls, which slowly tumbled down.

'I thought we were done with all that,' said Mary in an under-voice.

'It is only play, darling,' replied Henry. 'We are but playing, as children do; as we ourselves once did.'

'We are children no longer,' his sister replied, 'and our play-time is through.' Mary pinned up her hair again and made a great show of taking up her embroidery. 'Now that we are grown the risks are too great. I trust you take my meaning, sir.'

Henry stood and removed himself from

Mary's side. He paced back and forth before her. 'I see your friendship with Miss Price has had an effect. You are become like her—all prudishness and naïveté. Are you modest, Mary?'

Mary made no reply.

'How alike our loves are! Timid, meek, boring Fanny; proper, righteous, dreadful Edmund. It is *they* who belong together. Yes, it makes all the sense in the world.—Mary, I have quite an hypothesis; I aver Fanny and Edmund are already lovers! They are too much alike to have resisted the other. Do you suppose they could have staid in their own beds, night after night, these many years at Mansfield Park?'

Mary was caught between laughter and consternation. 'Henry, you have quite lost your mind. They are nearly brother and sister.'

'As we are the genuine article.'

Mary coloured, and fixed her eyes on her needlework; but her brother was again beside her. He took up his sister's hand that held the needle and kissed each finger. Mary was soon restored by this attention to her customary liveliness.

'Can you not imagine it?' he said, and then, in a very different voice: 'Fanny, how very . . . *pious* you look today.' Mary could not contain a burst of laughter. The voice was Edmund's. Her brother's imitation was superb—he had always been a marvelous actor, everyone said so.

Henry stood up and crossed the room with his back to Mary. He then turned around and approached her again. His face was changed; there was an innocence, or mock innocence, now inscribed upon it. He adopted a tentative, mincing step: the careful gait, cruelly exaggerated, of poor Edmund.

'My dearest Fanny,' entreated Henry, 'may I please read the truly dreadful and tremendously dull sermon I have prepared to give as my first at Thornton Lacy?'

'If you are going to force me into this little play, Henry, at least do it properly—without your horrid wit.'

'Yes, dear, of course. Let me start again.' Henry assumed a new air of seriousness and sincerity, and said again in uncanny imitation of Edmund's voice, 'My dearest Fanny, I beg your pardon, but I wished to consult you about the sermon I've been attempting to write these past weeks. I would be forever grateful if you would give me your kind assistance.'

'It would very much please me to do so.' The voice was Fanny's, or near enough; Mary had some of her brother's gift of mimicry.

'(Very nice dear, I almost believed it was my *objet* herself speaking; you have that particular drop of her head.) Thank you, Fanny,' he replied with a look of meaning, 'I feel that your natural delicacy will help tranquillise my anxieties. You are so good. May I take the seat next to yours?' Mary lowered her head even further, in a silent, subdued moue. 'Dear Fanny, would it trouble you if I held your hand while I read to stem my agitation?'

Mary managed a true blush and turned away with a look of excessive agitation. 'Sir, you are sitting within eighteen inches of me! You have exceeded the proximity, delineated clearly by all the best moral guides, beyond which a gentleman must not venture with regard to a lady!' Mary stood up, feigning the desire to flee.

'Oh Fanny, do not go. We are such good friends. May not we venture within eighteen inches?'

'Very well; eighteen, but no closer.'

'Not seventeen?' replied Henry, moving closer.

'Edmund!' Mary cried, in mock agitation.

'We are like brother and sister—what could possibly be wrong?'

Mary affected to consider this, before rising and placing herself, with her head bowed, upon her brother's lap. As Edmund, Henry became highly flustered; for himself, he was most gratified, and physically not unmoved.

'My dearest Fanny, you surprize me.'

'Oh Edmund! My self-governance is gone. In your presence, I have no humility. You are so good, and I am wicked; I am evil.'

'Be soft with yourself. You are not capable of evil. You are true goodness, Fanny; that is your whole.'

'No, you do not know me, Edmund—you

do not know what fills me.' Mary paused, blushed again, and cried out, 'Edmund, I confess, when I am up in the school-room, I think of you. When I am reading Cowper, I think of you. When I am ministering to the poor in the village, when I am copying virtuous quotations into my commonplace-book—'

'Fanny, say no more!' cried Henry. 'There can be but one course of action open to us. Let us pray. Let us open our hearts to God.'

They knelt chortling on the floor before the sofa, and, clasping their hands before them, began to utter whatever scraps of prayer they could remember from their childhood. These were not much, and soon both were laughing at how little of the language of virtue remained in their hearts and memories. They began instead to whisper anything that came to mind—nonsense words—the lyrics of bawdy songs—the sort of doggerel that sailors at sea could be flogged for reciting within the hearing of an officer.

On the floor, they were closer to the fire; and before long their mock-reverent exertions had made them warm. The room was still frightfully stuffy; and it occurred to both to loose their clothing. They did, assisting one another, and for several moments neither spoke. Then, again in Fanny's voice, Mary said, 'Edmund, you are now much closer than eighteen inches.'

'I calculate I am exactly eight inches away from you, Fanny.'

'More like five.'

'Six, then.'

'Oh, do what you will with me, Edmund; I put myself entirely in your kind hands!'

'You know I have never been with a woman, Fanny. I know not what to do. Please help me to know what you would like of me.'

'I am timid, Edmund; I am unlike other people; speech does not come easy,' Mary replied shrinkingly.

'I will attempt to forge ahead, if you will not judge me.'

'I am not capable of judging one so dear to my heart. I am only sorry I am not more than I am; more capable of strength and fortitude.'

With great earnestness, Henry exulted, 'Fanny, do not speak ill of yourself. I have the deepest gratitude for any words you choose to share with me and if you choose silence, I will be eternally grateful for that as well, as long as we fear not, rather trust in the goodness of our natures, allow hope to lead us down the path of pure conscience, guide each other down the worthy road—'

'Edmund?'

'Yes, Fanny?'

'Why don't you put your hand here?' Mary pulled Henry's hand to her breast, now fully exposed.

'Oh, God! I am in raptures, Fanny. I feel a true ecstasy,' replied Henry with false heavy sighs.

Mary looked at her brother. 'Can you hold on to that ecstasy for a few moments longer, dear Edmund? Premature ecstasy is a sin no one should indulge.'

Henry now too dropped his assumed look of innocence and unalloyed sympathy, and resumed his customary leisurely arrogance. 'Mary, dear, you bestrode the line between what could be, and what could not, so perfectly; but now you have gone too far; you have revealed your true nature.'

'Are you saying, sir, that my skills as an actress have reached their limits?'

'No, Mary, you are a true talent,' said Henry, unbuttoning her further and putting his tongue to her ear.

In the throes of her lust for her brother, Mary said, 'Let us be expelled from all proper society. At least it will allow us to live the life we desire.'

'Do not make decisions in haste, dear. We have all the time in the world,' Henry replied.

'Then do me one turn for the present?' Mary asked, breathless, as she knelt in front of him and removed his breeches altogether.

'And what would that be?'

Mary looked up at her brother. 'Allow me to be the sole receiver of you. Fanny is not worthy of this grand instrument. It would not be right to inflict it upon her, Henry; and, moreover I am not prepared to give you up quite yet.'

'But my dear sister, I thought we were done with all this. Is that not so?' said Henry. Mary was receiving his very instrument in such a manner as prohibited any sort of response, so Henry continued. 'Were you not keen on putting an end to our activities? Please explain your unaccountable reversal.'

Mary momentarily paused her activities, though her handiwork withstood no interruption, and considered the question. 'I suppose, my dear brother, that I am merely evil to my core and have absolutely no hope of developing a moral bone in my body. I allow it was pleasant to play at morality and goodness; but now let us put virtue away, as we put away all childish things. I will only add, Henry, that I hardly need your mocking censure.'

And without attempting any further remonstrance, she took her brother to the height of bliss and *left Fanny to her fate.*

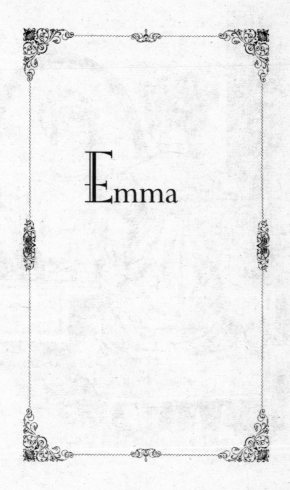

Emma

There was nothing Emma liked less than to have to witness herself in an uncontrolled state . . .

Emma Alone

Austen's delightfully self-absorbed, self-satisfied, and self-deluding heroine is still in the early stages of her education in the following missing scene that appears to be the original Chapter 10. Little has occurred to anguish her vanity or to convince her that any other person is quite as important as herself. As Emma says, 'My being charming, Harriet, is not quite enough to induce me to marry; I must find other people charming—one other person at least.'

Emma has just come from an encounter with Mr. Elton, the new vicar, and Harriet, the rural innocent whom Emma has adopted as a protégée. Mr. Elton is in love with Emma—but Emma thinks he loves Harriet, and that she has succeeded in cementing a match between them. In Chapter 9, we leave Emma gleeful and laughing over her supposed accomplishments. To the satisfaction she feels on the subject, she now adds another kind.

Chapter 10

Emma soon found herself sitting in her dressing closet as she finished off her hearty laugh. Calmed, she peered smiling at herself in the looking-glass and said aloud, 'You are quite a woman, Emma. Your virtue is even more than you were wont to believe. Excellent work you have done. Cleverer than your keenest admirers would even suppose. And Mr. Knightley can now begin to compose his apologies. Well done, Emma, well done.'

Emma could not remove the smile from her face, pleased as she was with herself. Again and again, she rehearsed in her mind how perfectly in the right she was in designing such a match between Harriet and Mr. Eliot. Her judgement would soon be lauded by all. Emma's elegant manner would, of course, induce her to deny all praise—at first. But, she would slowly allow for a compliment here and there; remarks upon her foresight, assistance, intelligence, advice and general good will would be allowed, in bits and bites now and again, especially in Mr. Knightley's presence—to be sure he was made to understand exactly how right she was.

'How very hard it is to be Miss Emma Woodhouse,' she thought. 'Not even Mr. Knightley, gentleman that he is, can claim to have the sort of quickness and powers of assistance as I. Though I have no peers, it is a comfort to know what comfort I bring to others. I can be satisfied with that, if nothing else.'

This self-praise was just the sort of wood for Emma's fire. For one who seee herself as superior to all, there is nothing quite as rousing as a compliment from oneself. Emma continued in this manner for some time, as she was in the habit of doing—for hours at a time—since little other activity was nearly as captivating to her attention. Soon she was quite breathless with hearing so much unqualified approbation. Emma looked at her rosy complexion, touched her fingers to her lips to kiss them, and then moved her fingers to those very same lips facing her in the looking-glass. 'For you, Miss Woodhouse' she said aloud.

Emma continued to observe herself; every detail of her eyes, nose, lips, hair, neck, bustline. Her smile grew as she took in more and more of herself. 'What a fine figure you cut—the finest in Highbury, if not in all of the county!' she thought with bravado.

Emma removed her glove and moved her hand up under her shift as she continued her imaginings. Each thought brought a new wave of pleasure and heightened good looks. Emma was not the sort to allow an activity that accentuated any one of her numerous assets to pass her by; and so she continued to form a list of her accomplishments without hesitation.

'Miss Taylor at Randalls—my doing,' brought on a deep sigh.

'And now Harriet at the vicarage—my doing.' Emma closed her eyes and laughed as she reached further under her dress.

'Chusing the perfect fabric for my new parasol to wear with my lemon yellow poplin frock—only I would have seen the match in the two.' She bowed to herself and let out an elegant little cry.

'Mr. Knightley's heartfelt amends followed by a remorseful session of praise.' Emma could hardly stand the excitement such thoughts produced. She moved her hand out from under her to take in the fragrance of herself with fervish delight. 'As always, smelling and tasting like lilies of the valley with a hint of lavender.' Emma dipped back under her dress where her activity resumed with some fervour. She thought momentarily of her needing to get everything in order for dinner, but did not allow this thought to interrupt her activities. Rather, it heightened her excitement as it reminded her (not that she ever truly forgot) of how essential she was to the flawless running of the household. It would do to have her father and Harriet take a moment without her if only to realise how utterly necessary she was to them in every way. Of course, they were surely already convinced of this matter, but Emma believed one could never feel too much her usefulness.

Before long, Emma was near completely done with her regalement. At this point, she did what she always had done—stopt; for small beads of perspiration began to appear on Emma's brow and her colour deepened from a

rosy blush to a coarse crimson. There was nothing Emma liked less than to have to witness herself in an uncontrolled state—not that she had
ever observed such a state in her person; such
inelegance and bad taste were not a part of her
existence. But, she certainly was not willing to
risk any behaviour of the sort; she would leave
that to those of inferior habits. One ought to
know how to conduct oneself with decorum at
all times and in all circumstances; moreover, to
have the ability to control oneself was yet
another reason to be pleased with oneself, or so
Emma believed.

And so Emma congratulated herself, once
again, for her complete self-command. She
carefully arranged her dress, dabbed her brow,
and observed her visage in silence as she
thought, 'What an honour to be me.'

Nothing like a little buggery to spice up a morning.

Knightley and Churchill

This missing scene was to be the original Chapter 42 of *Emma*. In Chapter 41, Mr. Knightley speculates on Frank Churchill's double-dealing with respect to Emma and Jane Fairfax, and Mr. Knightley's fury with Frank Churchill peaks.

Why the wise, steady Knightley's feelings are so aroused by the apparently amiable Frank Churchill is a bit of a mystery in the novel. As Austen writes, "Mr. Knightley, who, for reasons best known to himself, had taken an early dislike to Frank Churchill, was only growing to dislike him more." The "lost" scene makes his motives far more clear.

Mr. Knightley returned to Donwell Abbey in an ill-humour. Unable to sit and settle his accounts, he decided to play a game of billiards. It was by no means his usual activity, but he was intent on reviewing the day's disquieting events. That something had transpired between

Frank Churchill and Jane Fairfax, he felt sure. Their behaviour earlier that evening was a testament to attachment—of what sort, he did not know—nor would he wish to, were he not concerned for Emma. Her ill-treatment was foremost in his thoughts as he pondered the many suggestions of Frank Churchill's duplicity.

It was in the middle of these thoughts that Mr. Frank Churchill himself was announced. In a rare moment of confusion, Mr. Knightley stammered and finally communicated his consent for his guest to be brought forward.

Frank entered, and they stood together in the billiard-room. Mr. Knightley muttered a greeting and then began to play in order to compose his thoughts. Frank Churchill declined to join in the game (though he was not asked), preferring, he said, to watch. It was a situation that inevitably demanded conversation, and Mr. Knightley was obliged to make some, little though he did desire it. He asked if the Westons made a safe return home, yet declined to ask why his visitor had come at all, as he did not wish to hear the answer. Frank

Churchill was not so restrained, and in a very short time had covered the weather, the state of his health, the health of a new hunter he had recently bought, the noise in London, the theatre in Bath, his new hair cut, Miss Fairfax's new pianoforte, Miss Fairfax herself, Miss Woodhouse's hair, and Miss Woodhouse, entire. All of these subjects were treated equally superficially, except the last, on which he lingered, saying how much he admired Emma—and what a fine girl she was—what a sharp wit—what lovely eyes, and on, and on. Soon Mr. Knightley felt he had to interrupt.

'You speak a great deal of Emma.'

'I think very highly of her,' Frank Churchill replied casually.

'And Miss Fairfax?'

'I think highly of her as well.'

'You show attention to them both,' Mr. Knightley replied with indignation, then checked himself. Emma had always tolerated his admonitions with good humour; Frank Churchill might not be so glad to receive them, and Mr. Knightley owned that he had perhaps become too accustomed to dispensing unasked-for wisdom. So he did not speak further, but only continued his game of billiards.

'You are thinking that I pay too much attention to either Emma, or Miss Fairfax, or both,' said Frank Churchill.

'I wonder that you should know so well what I was thinking.'

'Yes; yet may one not admire both? I like Miss Fairfax; I like Miss Woodhouse. Do you like my new hair cut?'

'We are not speaking of your hair cut, Mr. Churchill,' said Mr. Knightley.

'We were not speaking of it before, but now we are! Do you like it?' Frank Churchill asked.

'I had not formed an opinion of it,' replied Mr. Knightley gravely.

'I beg you to form one now, if it is not too much trouble.'

The man was too, too irritating. 'Very well, your hair cut looks well, though I wonder that you needed to go to London to get it.'

'There, you see?' said Frank Churchill.

'Now you are admiring *me*.'

'Sir, I most certainly am not!' cried Mr. Knightley.

'You have admired me, Mr. Knightley, just as I have admired Miss Woodhouse, and Miss Fairfax. It would be a shame, would it not, if one were limited as to the people in this world one could admire? I believe in variety in all things. Now, Mr. Knightley, you must let *me* admire *you*.' And he took the billiard-cue from Mr. Knightley's hand. Mr. Knightley was too surprized to stop him; and now stood, frozen, his mouth open in wonder, the arm that had held the billiard-cue still outstretched.

'A most admirable pose, one that shows you to distinction,' said Frank Churchill, who proceeded to enumerate Mr. Knightley's many little elegancies of form and dress, speaking with particular relish of Mr. Knightley's bear-ing ('How very fine is your posture, sir! How rigid and erect!'), and Mr. Knightley's breeches, which Frank Churchill admired for their snugness.

This man is absurdly promiscuous in his

affections, thought Mr. Knightley. That he should flirt openly with Miss Woodhouse while his affections lay also with Miss Fairfax, was bad enough; that his attentions should fall on Mr. Knightley himself was too much to stand!

At least, however, Frank Churchill had left off cataloguing him, and was now occupied with examining the billiard-cue, and running his fingers along the length of it. 'I have never played billiards,' he said. 'I have never learnt how, and have been often at a disadvantage as a result. Sir, would you be so kind as to show me how to manipulate this wonderfully long and admirably smooth weapon?'

Mr. Knightley was provoked exceedingly. 'Alas, I have just recollected a most pressing appointment. I must say good-bye to you, sir.'

'Perhaps some other time?' Mr. Churchill asked.

'I fear I would make a very poor instructor.'

'Some other sport, then? Riding?'

'Alas, no,' was Mr. Knightley's decidedly short answer.

'I enjoy bathing.'

'I do not, sir.'

'Greco-Roman wrestling? I can bring the oil.'

'Good day to you, sir,' Mr. Knightley replied, sharply.

But, Frank Churchill was not to be put off easily. He acted as if only the most innocent of pleasantries had been exchanged and sat languidly in an arm-chair.

Mr. Knightley knew not what action to take. That their connexions made it unthinkable to eject Frank Churchill from his house was evident; yet, Mr. Knightley would not sit back and take the conceited sport of his guest. 'Mr. Churchill, I have wished you good-day and yet you sit, unmoved. I would ask you where, in this situation, one could find your merit if I believed there was any merit to be had, but I will not look for what does not exist. Thus let me simply inform you that you will not finesse me nor use me ill as you have succeeded with so many others. If you chuse to sit here, it is a labour in vain. I will no longer idle with you in order to enhance your pleasure. Now, sir, I will retire to my library. You may remain in the billiard-room as long as you wish.' Mr. Knightley moved towards the doorway, but the younger and more agile Frank Churchill was too quick for him. He blocked the way out, saying, 'Ah, you have discovered my true object—the game of which I am truly fond! How did you know?'

'I care little for what you are fond of—sir, please move from the door.'

But Frank Churchill merely matched Mr. Knightley's steps so that the former continued to meet the latter face to face. Soon Mr. Knightley was crimson with vexation. "Sir, I will ask you once more to please remove yourself from my path.'

'And if I do not?' Frank teazed. 'You cannot hide your pleasure from me, dear sir. I feel your temperature rising already and I have not even laid a finger on you.' With this, Frank Churchill slid his finger up Mr. Knightley's torso. 'It's hard to imagine how I long for you. Would you like to know the exact dimensions of my longing?'

'What is it that you want?' said Mr. Knightley in a flush of confusion and, to his great displeasure, stimulation.

'Isn't it obvious what I want?' Frank Churchill retraced the path of his finger, only this time moving some distance below his point of origin. 'I'll give you a hint in the form of a charade.'

'I want no charade, sir.'

'Yes, I see what you want.' Frank looked down. 'But do indulge me, Mr. George Knightley—for you have very little choice.'

Mr. Knightley resigned himself to the whim of his guest, but not without gathering himself first. He saw through Frank Churchill and would not fall prey to his gallantry and trick.

'I have been awaiting the chance to puzzle you for some time now, Mr. Knightley. I have had so little time to compose—you see I came here most unexpectedly, out of restlessness, not planning. I am sure you know the sort of state I am referring to.'

'No, I am afraid I do not.'

'Unimportant, really. Right then, here it is:

I will tell you now
 for all 'tis worth
you are looking for
 a patch of earth.

With exclamation
 to the letter
Not myself *nor* I
 could do better

It is the first of three
 that tells this tail *(a pun—or rather a*
clue, sir, that you shall see when I write it down)
 and completes the word
 to great avail!'

Mr. Knightley, though little interested or experienced in puzzles, was adept at figuring them. The first stanza was the most difficult. 'A patch of earth'—was it a divot?—or was it sod? The next two lines were clearly the letter 'o' and the next two could only be 'me'—'o-me.' Mr. Knightley tried putting the three together: 'divot-o-me.' It made no sense. He replaced 'divot' with his second thought and tried again.

To say he was stunned, to say he turned pale with horror, would not capture Mr. Knightley's reaction. He could not speak— could hardly fathom how he had allowed this sort of disgrace to take place in his own home.

At last, with a composed asperity, Mr. Knightley said, 'You must leave this instant, Mr. Churchill. I withstood your insults in duty to my friends, but I will have your insolence no longer. You stand on no moral ground, thus I can share no conversation with you. And I will add, I have the law of the land behind me, sir.'

'You are offended by my charade? Do you mean to tell me, in all honesty, that you have not engaged in such activity? Were you not at school?'

Mr. Knightley went to ring the butler when Frank stopped him by rising from his seat. 'Yes, I know when I am no longer wanted. I am to see our beloved Emma, first off tomorrow. I shall have to put the charade in her friend's book! Nothing like a little buggery to spice up a morning. Though sadly 'tis only in words.' With this, Frank departed and all of Mr. Knightley's suspicions were confirmed; Frank's character was as ill—more ill, more reprehensible—than even he had supposed. Now he had only the unpleasant task of cautioning Emma.

Northanger Abbey

Miss Morland, the apparatus are mine.

Henry and Catherine

In *Northanger Abbey*, Catherine Morland is invited to stay at the eponymous estate by her new friends, the attractive Henry and Eleanor Tilney. A serious fan of gothic novels, Catherine becomes intrigued by Henry, the mysterious house, and the even more mysterious General Tilney, who Catherine comes to believe murdered Henry and Eleanor's mother.

That all of Catherine's fantasies turn out to be false is part of Austen's satire of gothic conventions—but it is also, on a narrative level, a bit disappointing, since every spooky room in the Abbey turns out to be empty; every sinister gesture of the General's, harmless.

As the lost scene below shows, though, one of Catherine's fantasies did eventually come to be realized.

. . . *It was done; and Catherine found herself alone in the gallery before the clocks had ceased to strike. It was no time for thought; she hurried on,* slipped with the least possible noise through the folding doors, and without stopping to look or breathe, rushed forward to the one in question. The lock yielded to her hand, and luckily, with no sullen sound that could alarm a human being. On tip-toe she entered; the room was before her; but it was some minutes before she could advance another step. She beheld what fixed her to the spot and agitated every feature.——She saw a large, well-apportioned apartment, an handsome dimity bed, arranged as unoccupied with a handmaid's care, a bright Bath stove, mahogany wardrobes and neatly-painted chairs, on which the warm beams of a western sun gaily poured through two sash windows! Catherine had expected to have her feelings worked, and worked they were. Astonishment and doubt first seized them; and a shortly succeeding ray of common sense added some bitter emotions of shame. She could not be mistaken as to the room, but how grossly mistaken in everything else!—the General must be entirely blameless—there was nothing here—unless—

With fear of discovery still upon her, she decided to examine the wardrobe more closely. It was as tall as she. She opened the drawers and found them empty. She now resolved firmly to quit the room—but not before making a quick inspection of the upper part of the wardrobe. She tried the doors—surely they would be locked—but they were not, instead they swung open with a creak when she tried them. What would she find within the mahogany wardrobe? Would it, too, be filled with cob-webs, or stored bedding, or yellowing laundry lists? A heroine of any merit must possess a vivid imagination and Catherine duly owned her part in this matter. I will let the reader decide whether our young lady's actions are defendable or whether a mind seduced by the pages of novels caused such reprehensible behaviour. Those who take the latter point of view, I believe, will fault her biographer as much as herself. Hence, I will take my heroine's part and allow her to continue her imaginings, even if disappointment follows as her only companion; for Catherine was indeed prepared for any further disappointment.

On beholding what lay within the wardrobe, her initial disappointment gave way to confusion. A number of objects were before her. Wondering, she took them out, one by one, and laid them on the nearest easy surface, which was the bed.

Catherine was a country girl, and like many very fond of riding. She had grown up with horses, and so she had seen many items similar, but not quite like, those which she now saw before her. There was something like a saddle, but much smaller, and with many more buckles and clasps, and without stirrups. There was something like a riding crop, but much thinner, and with—what? feathers?—affixed to one end. There was, oddly, a woman's corset, which Catherine saw was also fashioned from leather—leather! She coloured as she handled it, though she could not say, why this should be. There was a horse-whip. There were some coils of rope, of varying lengths and thicknesses. There were shackles fashioned, bafflingly, of red velvet. There was a pair of pattens.* There were several other objects which, apart from some

* Device worn on women's shoes on rainy days, consisting of a metal ring on small stilts, designed to keep the wearer an inch or so off the ground.

vague resemblance to both livery and haber-
dashery, Catherine could not categorize nor
identify.

She stood silent for a moment before the
bizarre assemblage, and tried to steady her rac-
ing thoughts. Vague as her notions were as to
the actual function of the implements before
her, their general purpose could not be
doubted. Here was the evidence she had sought.
The General was a murderer, or (this much was
certain) a bondsman and torturer of the most
sinister and perversely couture-oriented kind.

At that instant a door underneath was
hastily opened; some one seemed with swift
steps to be approaching the room in which
Catherine now stood. She had no power to
move. With a feeling of terror not very defin-
able, she fixed her eyes on the doorway, and in
a few moments it gave Henry to her view. 'Mr.
Tilney!' she exclaimed in a voice of more than
common astonishment. He looked astonished
too. 'Good God!' she continued, not attending
to his address. 'How came you here?—how
came you into this room?'

'How came I into this room!' he replied, greatly surprized. 'Because it is part of my father's house; and why should I not come into it?' He was about to make further inquiries, when his eyes fell upon the bed, and the collection of apparatus placed upon it by Catherine. For a moment he did not speak.

Catherine recollected herself, blushed deeply, and gave him to understand what had brought her to the room—there was no disguising the deed, there was only to explain it, and she did explain all—the intrigue the room held for her—her discovery of the objects in the wardrobe—her convictions as to their probable use by General Tilney—it poured out of her in a rush. She finished, breathless; and Henry fixed her with a stern gaze.

With fewer words than she had used to convey her suspicions, Henry began to dismantle them. Henry could scarce believe the notions she was entertaining. 'If I understand you rightly, you had formed a surmise of such horror as I have hardly words to—Dear Miss Morland, consider the dreadful nature of the suspicion that you have entertained. What have you been judging from? Remember the country and the age in which we live. Remember that we are English!'

'But did your mother not die suddenly? And did not your father—'

His father, he replied with some warmth, had loved his mother, who died of a sudden illness, attended by doctors of the most unassailable reputation. 'But these very sinister-looking objects—'

'They did not belong to my father,' Henry said. 'He does not even know they are here.'

'Then to whom do they belong?' Catherine cried.

'Miss Morland, the apparatus are mine.'

Catherine stared at him, unable to speak. What had she done? What must he think of her? She, who had all but accused his father of murdering his mother. Catherine held back tears of embarrassment and shame.

Henry sat down upon the bed. 'I can but wonder that you have attached a sinister purpose to my—well, let us call them my toys.'

'Toys?' Catherine cried.

'Yes—what word would you use, for that which provided hours of delight and enjoyment? Toys I suppose is as good a word as any other. Have you really no notion as to their purpose?'

'I thought I had, but it seems I was mistaken.'

'Indeed you were,' replied Henry. 'Do not be afraid, Miss Morland, there is nothing sinister here. Can you guess what my toys are for?'

Catherine thought of hunts, and riding, and obscure equestrian skills. 'Are they . . . for taking exercise?'

Henry smiled. 'Yes, of a sort. That is a very good way of putting it. Shall I show you?'

Catherine at once agreed; for, though she had not realised it until now, the many days spent indoors at Northanger Abbey had left her longing for exertion and fresh air. She began to quit the room, saying she must fetch her bonnet; but Henry stopped her, saying their exercise could be taken indoors, in this very room. He went on to explain, in the most gentle terms, and with all the simplicity and directness which Catherine had grown to admire so much in his character, the many and various functions of his toys, speaking with precision as to their modes of use, and with obvious affection of their high standard of workmanship and durability.

Many gentlemen had hobbies, Catherine knew; they occupied themselves with card-parties, or abusing the servants, or collecting bits of shells. Catherine disliked cards; they bored her, and natural history she found tedious. Most so-called hobbies were devised chiefly to consume both money and time, to name but two commodities enjoyed and wasted by the gentry in abundance. Or so Catherine reflected, with a sharp intake of breath, as Henry finished pulling tight the last of the laces on the leather corset, the corset she now wore. Though constricting, and rather stiff and creaky, she felt very suddenly, and to her surprise, that she preferred it to the muslins and silks she had worn all her life; indeed she felt, as Henry introduced the velvet shackles into her hand, a thrill of confidence and assurance unlike any she had previously known.

During her reverie he too had been at work upon his clothes, and Catherine was startled to find him completely altered, as he was both taller (as he was tottering, in his top boots, upon the pattens) and prettier (dressed as he was in Catherine's discarded muslin chemise and cotton cap).

'Miss Morland,' he said, 'we have both misbehaved. You by having entertained such suspicions of my family as led you to investigate this room without permission; I by having failed to bring you here myself, and long ago. Miss Morland, let us each atone for what we have done.'

They did; and Catherine began to learn a little of the penalties, and pleasures, that an inflamed imagination might produce.

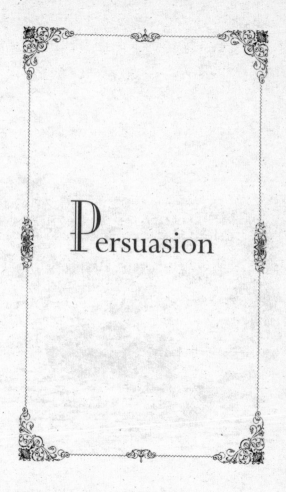

Persuasion

. . . the capacities and worthiness of the tiny rowboat were tested thoroughly . . .

Persuasion: The Prequel

We were initially puzzled by the manuscript pages from *Persuasion*. Like the "lost" passages from the other novels, they had clearly been cut for their explicitness, but we could not determine where they had been meant to fit into the original novel. Were they from *Persuasion* at all? Anne Eliot, Captain Wentworth, Anne's protector Lady Russell—all are familiar from the published version. But nothing else is.

Persuasion deals, of course, with the aftermath of a failed youthful romance between Anne and Wentworth. It takes place years after their painful breakup, and is about regret, growing older, second chances. In the newly discovered scenes, though, Anne is young; Captain Wentworth has yet to make his fortune; and both are wildly and, as you will see, passionately in love.

It quickly became clear that these are not excised scenes from *Persuasion* at all, but rather fragments from an entirely different, unfinished novel. Evidently Austen began writing the book in the richly erotic mode of which we now know her to have been a master; abandoned it, knowing it would never be acceptable to her publisher; and started over, setting the reconceived version—*Persuasion*—eight years later than the original material.

Here, then, are fragments from what must be called *Persuasion: The Prequel*.

~~~~~~

. . . Sir Walter was gratified, no less by the success of his party, than by the exquisite pleasure which his new long-coat afforded him. He had ordered it made for the occasion, and now, as he stood with Lady Russell observing the prospect which surrounded him, of his home filled with happy young people enjoying all the warmth which Kellynch Hall could offer, he could not help but glance at his own reflection in the large looking-glass which hung above the piano, and admire the flattering way the velvet coat gripped his shoulders—the shoulders, he reflected, of a much younger man; ten years younger, at least.

Observing his gaze fixed upon the mirror,

Lady Russell, standing beside him, thought to say, 'What a fine, well-built young man is here! How lucky we are to have him.'

'Fine I will allow,' Sir Walter replied carefully. 'Well built, it is not for me to say; but young?'

'Yes, very young; and with all the vitality and joy of youth.'

Sir Walter smiled. 'Lady Russell, how very kind you are. But let us not deceive ourselves; the man you observe is vital, yes; youth*ful*; his looks preserved far better than those of his contemporaries; but to call him very young is flattery to a man who needs none.'

In a different tone, Lady Russell said, 'Sir Walter, I am speaking of the young naval officer there; Captain Wentworth, I believe he is called.'

Sir Walter started, and looking again in the mirror, saw the man indicated, standing a short way behind him. He made a hasty reply to Lady Russell, saying that, yes, he knew she was speaking of the Captain; that indeed he was not certain of his age, he might be older, or younger, than she supposed; but Sir Walter allowed him to be a well-looking man, one who had escaped, at least for the present, the physical ill effects so common to a life at sea.

Lady Russell said, 'I wonder if he has been introduced to Elizabeth.'

Sir Walter considered this as he continued to regard Captain Wentworth, now speaking with Anne across the room. Yes, he was an impressive, tall, handsome man; certainly Elizabeth was at least his equal (for she was, after all, the favor-ite daughter of Sir Walter) in purely physical charms; certainly Captain Wentworth would be gratified by an opportunity to know the woman who was, for all practical purposes, the mistress of Kellynch Hall. It was true that Wentworth was no-one, a young navy officer, with no fortune. But he had every prospect in the world of acquiring one. He had youth, he had talent, and the good regard of his superiors; and above all, he had his looks to recommend him. In short, Sir Walter considered him a good match for his eldest daughter. 'I shall endeavour to make sure that they meet.'

However, this proved harder to arrange than he at first imagined. During the long night, and through many dances—indeed, every dance—Captain Wentworth's attentions were held by an Eliot; but it was Anne, not Elizabeth, who captivated him; Anne, not Elizabeth, with whom he staid in conversation until nearly three, long after most of the other guests had returned home. Anne! She was a healthy-looking girl, his father allowed, with much of the bloom of her youth still intact, and not-unpleasing, if undistinguished, features; but for Anne to be the favoured one, while her much handsomer sister, who felt a great deal more keenly all the honours and advantages due her as an Eliot and resident of Kellynch Hall, went wanting, seemed to her father very wrong indeed. He consoled himself with the thought that the flirtation he and Lady Russell had observed had been a passing thing, a mere evening's fancy, prompted more by Elizabeth's retiring early (she had been complaining of a sore foot) than by any particular charms of her sister's. . . .

[The following day, though, Sir Walter is proved wrong:]

. . . Anne was alone at Kellynch. Lady Russell was tired and had gone home to rest; Elizabeth and Mary were about some little errands in town; and Sir Walter had gone to London with a view to buying some very large, full-length mirrors which, he judged, would suit the walls of his library most happily once all the books were removed. The house was calm, and Anne looked forward to a half a day of quiet. She was surprized, therefore, to have a visitor announced.

It was Captain Wentworth! Anne's surprize was all the greater, and she could barely utter a few words of greeting. His own speech, however, was little affected: He hoped it was not inconvenient, but he was out riding and found himself not far from Kellynch; and thought to deliver a note, thanking the Eliots for the ball the night before, himself; and also hoped to inquire, whether Miss Elizabeth's foot was feeling any better; and he wished to thank Anne for the many hours of conversation he had enjoyed—there were many reasons for his visit.

His face was flushed, Anne saw; her own was scarcely less so. But her colour, unlike Captain Wentworth's, could not be attributed to exercise. To be standing thus together, in the doorway of her empty house, but hours after they had parted the night before, was unexpected, novel, thrilling. She wanted to ask him in. She could not; not with her father, her sisters, even Lady Russell, absent.

Captain Wentworth was all understanding. Would she at least walk him to the gate, where he had left his horse? Anne at once agreed.

As they proceeded through the grounds, Captain Wentworth noted with admiration all the many little elegancies of the estate, the shrubbery, the garden. The grounds of Kellynch were indeed fine. Sir Walter spent lavishly on them; in this, at least, his vanity had produced some positive benefit to something other than himself. Anne was glad that her companion approved. 'I feared, Captain Wentworth, that a naval officer, a practical man of action, would disdain shrubberies and flowers.'

'On the contrary,' he replied. 'It is because we live and work confined in cabins, hemmed in by wood and water, that the cultivated beauties of a garden or a view are so deeply gratifying. I admire especially your yew-trees on that hill. And is that not a pond beyond?'

Anne said that it was; and they resolved to make a small detour to see it.

As they walked, Captain Wentworth went on to say that he meant no disparagement of ship-board life. He loved it; but its rough joys needed to be contrasted, now and then, with the gentler pleasures of the countryside. Did Anne not agree?

Anne replied that she had no way to know. She had never been at sea herself; but she had known women (the wives of officers) who found ship passage tolerable, and even enjoyed it, once they grew accustomed to its rigours.

Captain Wentworth could not agree. The cabins were too small, he said; the food too coarse; the general atmosphere on board entirely unsuitable for ladies. He would not have a woman on a ship under his command; he was loath to bring them aboard; he would not do their gentle sex that injustice. Anne again demurred; and there the argument stood, as they reached the edge of the pond.

It was a small pond of about an acre, entirely man-made, which Sir Walter had periodically stocked with fish, though he rarely troubled himself to catch one. He had also had built on the side nearest to the house a boat mooring, with a row-boat tied up alongside. It was a small boat, and was not often used. Captain Wentworth exclaimed with surprize when he saw it. 'A boat! A very handsome little boat! It has been a long time since I have rowed.'

Anne was still troubled by his previous remarks, and now made some further objections to them. Should not women be allowed to go to sea, if they wished? Particularly if a voyage were the only way to see their husbands? Should not their own testimony as to its merits be as admissible as Captain Wentworth's? She was bold enough to ask him this directly.

'Indeed,' he replied. 'You are right. There must be direct experience of the thing before any judgement is made. One of us may be wrong, or not; the only fault would be if we denied ourselves experience. Here we have a means of testing the proposition before us. Shall we go to sea?' And he indicated the row-boat.

Anne laughed, and was about to refuse. To sit in a boat with Captain Wentworth? It seemed entirely improper. But, as she considered, she saw that, while irregular, it could be no less correct than walking with him—for to be talking pleasantly together, while walking, or in a barouche, or in a boat—what could be the difference? And surely if she were to let herself be rowed, she could not pick a better oarsman than a Navy Captain; there would be no danger. And the boat sat too often idle. Like so many other extravagances of her father, it was purchased on a whim and since forgotten and neglected. It would be good to make *some* use of it.

Soon they were in the boat, and, propelled by a few long strokes of Captain Wentworth's, had pulled away from the dock.

'How do you find being at sea, Miss Eliot?'

'Most pleasant indeed, thank you, Captain Wentworth. I perceive nothing to dislike about it, so far.'

'Some ladies, I think, find the noise maddening; I mean the constant creak of wood and roar of waves.'

'I find it soothing,' Anne replied, smiling, 'and the sea-air most refreshing.'

'But what of the rolling of the boat? Some women never find their sea-legs. They are, indeed, so afflicted by the motion that they cannot leave their cabins to take the air; cannot eat; can scarcely talk.'

'The sea appears to me entirely calm today,' Anne said. Captain Wentworth was now steering the craft along the far shore, which was overhung with several ancient willow trees. He left off rowing, letting the oars sit idle in the water, and there they sat for several moments, speaking of very little, enjoying the weather and the fine surroundings.

'Miss Eliot, it appears I owe you an apology,' Wentworth said presently. 'Life aboard ship seems entirely to suit you.'

'Pray do not apologise, Captain Wentworth,' Anne replied. 'It is true I am happy at present; yet I cannot say, how I should feel were anything to happen to upset the tranquillity of the day, such as a storm, or an attack of privateers.'

At that moment, as if to answer her, the sun, which had been shining brightly, was obscured by a bank of cloud, one that appeared to stretch to the horizon. Captain Wentworth looked up to study the sky. 'You may get your storm, Miss Eliot. I cannot say about the privateers.'

They laughed, even as a chill gust of wind swept over them. A storm was indeed on its way. Anne ventured, that the Captain had best take them back to port. He agreed; and as he moved to take the oars again in hand another, entirely unexpected, gust of wind so shook the boat, that for a moment he lost his balance, and flailed his arms, and lurched, before landing awkwardly on the seat next to Miss Eliot.

He was embarrassed. Anne saw that he was embarrassed, and understood why he should be. A Navy Captain, the master of a sloop, who had battled storms and ships from the Channel to the West Indies, fumbling helpless in a tiny rowboat, on a lake that was scarcely a puddle, not four feet deep, and before a lady—this would be an embarrassment to him. For herself, Anne did not care—but she saw that *he* cared, and he saw that *she* saw; but it was with a smile that he then said, 'Now we see who has lost their sea-legs.'

Was it this joke, made at his own expense, and in such a spirit of good humour and honest self-appraisal, that so filled her heart with feeling, that she found herself, without entirely perceiving the moment of decision, with her arms flung around his neck, and her face tilted up to his? Was it her sudden gesture, so unexpected, and yet so desired (for he had desired it all through the hours of conversation and dancing the previous night, and on the long walk to the pond this morning, and in the boat) that caused him to bring his lips to hers? Was it the rain that, while never becoming quite a storm, began to fall steadily around them, which caused the

Captain to break off their embrace, if only long enough to bring the boat to harbour beneath the willow trees, where they could not be seen from the house, even had any one been at home?

Neither could have positively answered these questions in the affirmative; their thoughts were otherwise engaged.

Nor could they have said, whether their long discussion as to the difficulties of enduring life at sea, had much contributed, or had nothing at all to do with, the efforts of the next few hours, during which the capacities and worthiness of the tiny rowboat were tested thoroughly, and the proclivities of each, with regard to the gentle, rolling motion of a boat upon water, were established beyond a doubt.

All that is certain is that, some time later, the rain had stopped; the rowboat was again moored at its landing; Anne was returned to her home, and Captain Wentworth to his; and each was assured of their entire suitability to the other, and equally desirous of a life spent together, on sea or on land.

For Elizabeth, the day had not been nearly so gratifying. First, the shop in town had been out of the muslin she wanted. Then Mary, never the most agreeable of companions to begin with, had, on meeting a group of her friends in a tea-room, begun a seemingly endless and inane conversation, which ended only with Elizabeth's threat to leave her sister in town and return home alone, which she now was most desperate to do, owing to a return of the foot complaint which had kept her from dancing the night before.

Mary having called her bluff (saying she would be driven home by a friend), Elizabeth was now returning to Kellynch alone, early, and in a very foul mood. Her day in town was wasted; Mary was the rudest and most obstinate girl in the world; her foot hurt; and now it was raining, a hard, blowing rain that muddied the roads and slowed her carriage as it approached the house through the grounds.

It was while she was looking out the window at the sodden landscape, reflecting on her wasted day, and the wasted evening before, that Elizabeth noticed a peculiar feature in the landscape beyond. It was a boat. That ridiculous tiny row-boat of her father's, no longer moored in its proper place, but adrift and bobbing in the water along the far shore of the pond; bobbing most violently, she perceived.

The carriage path to the house did not wind very close to the pond at any point; but at its closest, which was where Elizabeth's barouche had now come, the road did come close enough, and the surrounding trees were spaced far enough apart, for Elizabeth to see, briefly but clearly, exactly what was happening upon the water.

Though it was the shock and disappointment of her life, she recovered quickly. And she as quickly resolved, that as soon as possible, if not sooner, she must have a conversation with her father.

The reader may easily imagine what followed. Elizabeth spoke with Sir Walter; Sir Walter spoke with Lady Russell; both then spoke with Anne. The message was brief. Anne must never again see Captain Wentworth. No-one in the family was to see him. The young man who, a few days before, had seemed so promising, such a fine match for Elizabeth, was now considered entirely unreliable and unsuited to marry even Anne. Anne's declaration, that Captain Wentworth had already made her an offer, and been accepted, drew only scorn. Her emphatic statements of her own hopes and wishes were met with calculations as to how they might be overturned. And overturned they were, swiftly, with a brief letter from Sir Walter to Captain Wentworth.

So was Elizabeth's disappointment turned to satisfaction; and so was Anne's happiness by the same means destroyed—she feared, forever.

The Watsons

(a butter churn, a poker, a mop-handle)

Richard Crosby's Editorial Comments

Austen's "unfinished" novel, *The Watsons*, has always proved a difficult puzzle for Austen scholars. What was Austen's vision for this work? How would her heroine come into her own? The new material shows that *The Watsons* was, in fact, a completed work, intended for publication by Austen, and summarily dismissed due to its content. The following letter was penned by the publisher who had promised to print *Susan* (later titled *Northanger Abbey*), but never did. We now know why the book never went to press and why only the beginning pages of *The Watsons* remain.

Madam,

When your brother first approached me with your manuscript for Susan, I believed I had come across a fine new lady novelist. Now I see how very mistaken I was. Your newest submission can only be called an abomination. That a lady would presume to write such depravity is beyond my comprehension. I would not believe it possible if certain turns of phrase did not incontrovertibly replicate your earlier work.

The Watsons, as you, madam, innocently title your vile creation, indeed had me intrigued up to Elizabeth's urging Emma to visit Croydon. As in Susan, your characters were admirably delineated, engaging and seemingly worthy of a tale. However, on Emma's arrival to Croydon, I was so appalled—so reviled—by the behaviour portrayed from this point to the very last line of the novel, I scarce have words to describe my disgust. I can only surmise, madam, that you have French blood coursing through your veins, and the very lowest of such blood at that. I will never be able to look at an innocent lamb in the same way again nor will a bonnet appear the benevolent object it has always been in my heart. No, both these and so many others (a butter churn, a poker, a mop-handle) are forever coloured in my mind.

To insure that no other eyes shall ever be forced to look upon these pages, I have taken the liberty, or rather upheld my duty, to burn everything but the first fifty pages—which were devoid of the filth that *follows*—*and return it forthwith to you, madam.*

My only happiness on this occasion is that delays early on in the process have not allowed for us to print Susan. Providence indeed works in miraculous ways. As you can surmise, madam, we will never be the conduit through which a word of your immoral pen be brought to the public, no matter how seemingly principled it may appear. I may have been fooled once, but I am not fool enough to be duped twice. May your work never see the light of day.

> *For R. Crosby & Co.*
> *I am,*
> *Richard Crosby*

Acknowledgments

I would like to extend my heartfelt thanks to the following people for their help with the documentation, analysis and publication of *Pride & Promiscuity*:

To Jamie Byng, the greatest publisher I have ever encountered by leaps and bounds, and to all the folks at Canongate. To Daniel Greenberg and James Levine of the Levine Greenberg Literary Agency for allowing me to take the original time off for an extended vacation to England. And for their continued support throughout the publishing process. To Joan Eckstut, Stan Eckstut, Kris Puopolo, Mark Gompertz, Melissa Rowland, Frances Rosenfeld, Michael Wright, Laura Sedlock, Jenny Weisberg, and Josh Shenk for their assistance in preparing the work. To renowned Austen scholar, Elfrida Drummond, who once and for all confirmed the authenticity of the documents and so graciously agreed to write the introduction to the book. Lastly, I would like to express my deepest gratitude to the one who deserves it most, Jane Austen.